———————— ★ ————————

A RELATIVE SITUATION

"Gillian, we need to sit down and have a good long talk. Why don't you stay with us tonight?"

"But Connie—"

"Annette is staying with Connie tonight," Michelle interposed silkily. "She won't be alone, if that's what you're thinking about."

"Well, yes, that was—"

"Don't worry, Gillian. We're not going to leave her by herself."

"In that case, I'll be glad to come. Thank you." Michelle murmured something and slipped away.

"That was smooth," Tom said, one eyebrow cocked.

I looked past his shoulder and saw Michelle whispering to her twin; Annette nodded once in response. "Yes, it was smooth," I replied. "They don't want to leave me alone with Connie."

Tom shot me a quick look. "You picked up on that, did you? Well, well. Does it begin to feel familiar?"

Being manipulated, he meant. And yes, it was beginning to feel familiar. I'd almost managed to forget how good the Deckers were at arranging everything exactly the way they wanted it.

———————— ★ ————————

BARBARA PAUL

IN-LAWS 'N' OUTLAWS

WORLDWIDE.

TORONTO • NEW YORK • LONDON
AMSTERDAM • PARIS • SYDNEY • HAMBURG
STOCKHOLM • ATHENS • TOKYO • MILAN
MADRID • WARSAW • BUDAPEST • AUCKLAND

IN-LAWS AND OUTLAWS

A Worldwide Mystery/September 1992

This edition is reprinted by arrangement with Charles
Scribner's Sons; an imprint of Macmillan Publishing
Company.

ISBN 0-373-26103-9

IN-LAWS
AND OUTLAWS

ONE

A CELEBRITY HAD DIED, an old Hollywood actress who was already a bit long in the tooth for the romantic leads she'd been playing back when I was a child. She'd gone on to character roles rather than retire, good for her, even garnering a supporting Oscar in her seventies. She'd ended up playing the grande dame (both on the screen and off) with a gusto that one could only envy, and her face and name were as familiar a part of moviegoers' lives as those of their own families. But at the age of eighty-eight her heart had simply given out; she'd come to Chicago to appear on some worthy telethon or other, still on the go, and had died in her sleep, in her hotel room. I was sorry she was gone. She'd made herself into a legend through sheer energy and will power, and now there was no one around to take her place; the lady was one of a kind. The obituary page offered a truncated version of her life; and then a new item began, headed *Death elsewhere*.

Isn't there always? I started to put the newspaper aside, but a name caught my eye.

Death elsewhere
Raymond Decker, 49, president of Decker and Kurland, a Boston-based venture capital firm with estimated assets of $600 million, died yes-

terday in a fire in his summer home on Martha's
Vineyard. Decker was the nephew of Congressman Oscar Ferguson of Massachusetts.

Investigators say Decker appeared to have
fallen asleep while smoking in bed. He was alone
in the house at the time of the fire.

Decker is survived by his wife, Connie, and two
sisters, Annette and Michelle. Decker's son Theo
was killed by kidnappers four years ago in a case
that made headlines throughout the world.

The family is planning a private service.

Oh dear god. Raymond was dead.

I couldn't believe it. Somehow I'd thought of Raymond Decker as one of those people who go on forever, part of that indestructible breed that survives
everything . . . earthquakes, pestilence, plagues of lo-
custs. Men like Raymond didn't die in accidents; they
died in battle, or in bed of old age after winning all
their battles. Causing his own death by smoking in
bed? That was in the same realm of absurdity as the
unstoppable Alexander the Great's choking to death
on a chicken bone. And poor Connie—first her only
child, and now her husband; that was enough to crush
a spirit far stronger than sweet, vague Connie Decker's.

Several things occurred to me at once. No mention
of Stuart, for one. And why hadn't Raymond just
walked out of the house when he realized it was on
fire? He must have been drinking, or perhaps he was
on medication that made him stuporous. What a
foolish way to die, and how horrible . . . burned alive,

my god. Nobody deserved to go like that, and certainly not Raymond Decker.

The venture capital firm of Decker *and Kurland*, the paper said. So Rob had finally made partner; lord knows he'd wanted it long enough. I wondered what had made Raymond change his mind; the Deckers didn't share the wealth lightly, but of course Rob had married a Decker.

And of course none of them had bothered to notify me.

I pulled open the bottom drawer of a file cabinet and rummaged through an assortment of papers and doodads I could never decide what to do with. There it was: an old address book I'd been on the verge of throwing out for years. I'd kept my life separate from that of the Deckers ever since Stuart died, but I could never bring myself to sever the connection irrevocably. I looked up Connie Decker's number in Boston.

But once I had the number, I hesitated. Of all the Decker clan, Connie was the one I'd known least well. I remembered her mainly as the accommodating wife, thoroughly overshadowed by all the strong personalities around her. Whenever I'd talked to her, she'd merely smiled and nodded at whatever I said. Not unreachable, exactly, but vague and distant—her defense system, when she didn't know how to respond to people. Just thinking about talking to her again made me a little uneasy. But then I was ashamed of myself; the woman had lost her husband, for god's sake. Make the call.

Was she at home? It was more than likely Connie would be staying with some other member of the

family. She could even be at Martha's Vineyard; the
paper didn't say whether the fire had destroyed the
house or not. But no, she wouldn't be on the island;
not so soon after Raymond had died there. There was
only one way to find out; I tapped out her Boston
number.

An unfamiliar female voice answered and asked my
name when I said I wanted to talk to Connie. "I'll
have to ask her," the unidentified woman said.
"Connie hasn't been taking many calls." *Connie*, she
said—a friend or neighbor, then, not a servant. After
a moment, whoever she was came back and announced, "Connie says she doesn't know any Gillian
Clifford."

My mouth turned dry; I should have expected that.
"Tell her Gillian Clifford Decker."

In a matter of seconds Connie was on the phone.
"Gillian? Is that you?"

"It's me, Connie. How—"

"Oh, my goodness, *Gillian!*" Her voice was high
and she spoke in a rush, running her words together.
"It's been so long... I, I didn't recognize your last
name, I'm sorry, I'm in a bit of a muddle right now. I
should have known, even 'Gillian' should have told
me, I mean, how many Gillians do I know, you're the
only one, Raymond said it was appropriately theatrical—oh, Gillian, I'm so glad you called!" Her laugh
was skitterish and artificial. "You're just the—I mean,
I want to, ah, well, I don't even know where you're
living now!"

"Chicago. Connie, are you all right? You don't
sound so good. You sound..."

"Crazy?" The artificial laugh again. "That's what Rob told me. Well, not in so many words, but you know Rob, you know how he can say a thing by talking around it, you know?" I could hear her taking a deep breath. "Slow down, Connie," she told herself. "Gillian. Can you come to Boston? Please?"

I hadn't expected *that*. "Ah...when's the funeral?"

"Not for the funeral—oh, it's tomorrow, yes, come for the funeral, do." As if it were a tea party. "But, but...I need to talk to somebody who knows the family as well as you do but who isn't, well, caught up in it, if you know what I mean. Everybody here, they just say I'm in shock and time will help and all the other things people say to you when they want you to shut up. They just don't *listen*! Nobody listens."

This wasn't like Connie; she never talked this much, or in quite this way. "They don't listen to what?"

There was a pause. "Do you know how Raymond died?"

"The paper said he was smoking in bed and set fire to the house."

"That's such a convenient answer, isn't it?" Her voice was bitter. "Raymond had stopped smoking, months ago."

Oh dear. "I stopped smoking four times myself," I said as gently as I could.

"Meaning he backslid? But even if he did, he wouldn't have been smoking in bed. Gillian, Raymond didn't even smoke in the bed*room*. Never. He was always very considerate about that."

"But if you weren't there—"

"It wouldn't have made any difference. He still wouldn't smoke in the bedroom—he never did. You know how smoke lingers, gets in the drapes and the furniture. He just never smoked there."

"Well, then, the police made a mistake. Something else caused the fire."

"Some*body* else caused it."

It took me a few seconds to understand what she was saying. "Connie! You can't mean that!"

"Well, what else am I supposed to think?" She sounded close to tears. "First Theo...when the kidnappers, they..." Then suddenly she *was* crying. "And Bobby was next and then Ike and then it was Lynn, and now it's Raymond's turn, and—"

"Wait a minute, wait a minute—what about Bobby and Ike and Lynn?"

She made a keening sound. "You didn't know? You really didn't know? They're dead, Gillian! All three of them! And they all died this year!"

I was shocked speechless. Two nephews and a niece, none of them out of their teens...all dead within the past few months? When I could speak again, my voice came out almost as high and as strained as Connie's. "But how? Were they together? Did they—"

"Will you come?" she blurted.

"Yes, of course I'll come—I'll get a plane tonight. Do you have someone to stay with you? Who answered the phone?"

"That was Marcie—she says she'll stay as long as I need her."

Good for Marcie, whoever she was. "I'll call you back when I've made a plane reservation. I'll be there as soon as I can possibly manage it. Connie . . . hang on."

"Yes." She sounded exhausted.

Before I could think better of it, I told my secretary to book me on an evening flight to Boston. Then I called in my assistant and told him he'd be running the museum for the next few days. Then I shut everybody out of my office and let it all sink in.

Bobby. Ike. Lynn. Three bright and outgoing kids, with the whole world before them, their futures full of promise. Bobby and Lynn would have been starting college this fall, if my arithmetic was right; Ike was . . . a year younger? About that. What could have happened to them? With Theo dead at the hands of his kidnappers four years earlier, almost the entire younger generation of the Decker family had been wiped out. Only Joel Kurland was left, Bobby's younger brother. Fourteen or fifteen by now. My god. What happens to a family when all its young people die? Only young Joel was left to keep the family viable.

And it was my family, in a way. I had been a Decker for just a little over two years. At that time Theo, Raymond and Connie's only child, had still been alive and was clearly emerging as the leader of his generation of Deckers. That seemed only fitting, since his father had been the leader of his. Raymond was a good man, dynamic and likable if a trifle restricted in his view of the world, but with the head for business his younger brother so clearly lacked. Stuart, overflowing with charm and energy and self-confidence, wanted to be an actor.

He was the first Decker ever to show any interest in the professional theater, probably because the rest of them had enough high drama in their daily lives to keep them satisfied. No one in the family had tried to discourage him, as far as I could tell; I got the impression they were all amused by Stuart's yearning for something more exotic than high finance and sincerely wished him well. I first met Stuart when I cast him in a play I was directing in a Broome Street church basement, in one of those Manhattan neighborhoods it's generally best to avoid. The play was a pretentious piece of nonsense, but we didn't know that at the time; we were all still young enough that we hadn't lost our eagerness or our idealism, and we thought we could do anything. Stuart had wonderful stage presence; he wasn't so great on discipline, but he knew how to reach an audience. He just might have made it, if he'd lived long enough.

Only after Stuart and I had married did I start to understand what it meant to be a Decker. An only child of an only child of an only child, I had a little trouble getting used to having so much family around me all the time; sometimes I felt I was drowning in Deckers. But they were perceptive people and made it as easy for me as they could, the way they did with everyone who married into the family. And that's what you did when you married a Decker; you didn't marry just *that* Decker, you married the family.

You couldn't make it as a Decker without an extraordinarily strong sense of family; Deckers-by-marriage-only like me learned that rule pretty fast. Even semibohemian Stuart never seriously considered living his life without the rest of the clan to fall back on whenever it suited him. I think I was a little envious of them, of their unlabored closeness and their easy assumption that any member of the family had the right to ask any other member of the family for help when help was needed. "A place to go to recharge your batteries," Stuart had once said to me.

Stuart and Raymond's parents were dead, but the two brothers had two sisters who were very much a part of Decker life. Annette and Michelle were twins, the *twinniest* twins you could imagine. They shared everything, and I do mean everything. No, they didn't dress alike or play tricks on people; I doubted whether they'd done that even as children. But they thought the same things and did the same things; they were in complete harmony about everything in the world, and I never saw one spark of rivalry between them. They didn't know which of them had been born first, for their parents had never told them. Oh, I suppose they could have consulted hospital records or asked the doctor who delivered them; the fact that they never did suggested they liked not knowing which of them was the elder, even if only by minutes. Now in their forties, they were undoubtedly the same competent, self-assured women I'd known years earlier. Annette and Michelle were one person in two bodies—a trifle absurd in middle-aged women, perhaps, but there it was.

Annette had married a cardiac surgeon, Dr. Thomas Henry, and it was their son Ike who'd been one of the three youngsters to die earlier in the year. Ike had inherited the Decker genes—black hair and eyes, a body that was tall and slender. Annette took it for granted that one day young Ike would join the family business, but Dr. Tom wasn't so sure; Ike had started showing an interest in science at an exceptionally early age. Annette herself had gone to work in the firm as soon as her education had been completed.

So had Michelle; the venture capital firm of Decker and Kurland trusted their own. The "Kurland" part came from Michelle's husband, Rob, who'd married not only into the family but into the family business as well. Rob would not be in sole charge now that Raymond was dead, because the twins had long been equal partners. Technically, I suppose the firm should have been called Decker, Henry, Kurland, and Kurland— brother Raymond, sister Annette, sister Michelle, and husband Rob. But the twins made sure outsiders always understood they were Deckers; they'd introduce themselves by saying *I'm Annette Decker Henry* or *This is my sister, Michelle Decker Kurland.* Michelle and Rob were the parents of Bobby, so recently and so surprisingly dead, and Joel, the sole survivor of that ill-fated generation.

The last dead youngster was Lynn Ferguson, the daughter of Aunt Elinor and Uncle Oscar. Elinor was the Decker, Raymond and Stuart and the twins' aunt but only eight years older than Raymond. She'd married late, with the result that her daughter Lynn had been born the same year as Bobby Kurland, her niece Michelle's child. Elinor's choice of husband had been Oscar Ferguson, a Massachusetts state senator at the time; Decker money and influence had helped put Oscar in the U.S. House of Representatives. The Fergusons divided their time between Washington and

Boston, and like all the other members of the Decker clan spent part of every summer at Martha's Vineyard.

The last time I'd seen young Lynn Ferguson she'd been engaged in a half-teasing, half-serious argument with Bobby Kurland over whose turn it was to take the wheel when their Uncle Raymond took the sailboat out that day. That was my last summer at the Vineyard, not more than six months after Stuart had been struck down by a speeding van that never stopped to see if help could be rendered to a dying man. The entire Decker clan all the way down to young Joel had opened their arms and hearts to me even while struggling with their own shock and grief. They couldn't have been less selfish in their concern; I was made to understand I would always have a home and a family to support me.

How easy it would have been! That last summer on Martha's Vineyard I felt myself burrowing deeper and deeper into the family cocoon, letting Raymond and the others make my decisions for me, taking it for granted that I was included in all the Decker plans for the future. That sense of safety and of being looked after by those capable of doing the job properly can work as an anaesthetic; I was being numbed into the same lethargic, why-think-about-it state that had made Connie Decker so passive and do-less. I looked at Connie and I looked at me; I couldn't see much difference.

Fortunately, I had the same itch that Stuart had had; I woke up one morning realizing how desperately I missed the theater. I missed its excitement and its uncertainties; I missed *doing* things. I couldn't just sit still and be taken care of the rest of my life, as enticing as that prospect might appear. I had to go back. But I knew I could never divide myself between theater work and Deckerdom the way Stuart had done; I couldn't function under the burden of a split allegiance. It had to be a clean break.

So I told everyone goodbye and headed back to New York. It was a struggle; it's amazing how fast people can forget your name in that town. I did my best, but my best turned out to be not quite good enough. I did not become the hottest director on Broadway. Hollywood did not clamor for my services. I did get a job with a State Department goodwill tour, directing a theater group that traveled in China for four months. Then for a while after I got back, I worked for an agent, scouting off-Broadway productions in the hopes of finding publishable plays. Eventually I ended up in my present position, running a smallish theater museum in Chicago. My dreams of Tonys and Oscars were over; they'd never been very realistic dreams anyway. But I'd had my shot. And I didn't regret one minute of it; I wouldn't have missed it for the world. Also, I liked the work I was doing now; all in all, I was reasonably content.

I was content, that is, until I looked at the obituary page of the Chicago *Sun-Times* and its notice of *Death elsewhere* caught my eye. Going back into the Decker world wouldn't be easy under any circumstances, but on the heels of so many tragedies it just might prove impossible. But Lynn Ferguson had been my niece too, and Bobby Kurland and Ike Henry had been my nephews. I needed to find out what happened to them.

My secretary came in to tell me I was booked on a 6:10 flight to Boston. I gave her Connie's number and had her make the call; Connie's near-hysteria and half-formed accusations had gotten to me. Some*body* had set fire to the house on Martha's Vineyard, she'd said. In effect, she was saying Raymond Decker had been murdered.

If I were to catch a 6:10 flight, I needed to go home and pack. I notified one of the security guards I was leaving and passed four schoolgirls salivating over a gown Katharine Cornell had worn when she'd played Juliet in Chicago. I'd steadfastly resisted the use of docents ever since I took charge of the museum. Guided tours had their place, but people should be allowed to linger in a theater museum. Especially this one; Chicago had once been a big theater town, a worthy rival to New York. It wasn't now, of course, and hadn't been for some time; but its theater history was worth preserving.

Stuart hadn't been the least interested in the theatrical past; for him everything had to be *right now*—a vicarious rebellion against so much family tradition? Possibly he was just sowing wild oats, as the Deckers might see it, and eventually would have settled down in the family business. But I didn't think so. Stuart honestly loved performing on a stage, and he had a way of making a restless audience fall silent when he was speaking that is always the mark of the truly gifted. No, Stuart belonged on a stage, not in an office making money. There were enough other Deckers with that particular talent; the family business could get along perfectly well without Stuart.

But Stuart was dead, and I had broken off with my in-laws years ago to keep from being suffocated with kindness. Yet they'd stood by me when I needed them, and now they were the ones with trouble. If Connie Decker needed someone to talk to, then I would listen as long as she wanted me to.

TWO

In the cab from Logan Airport I began to get cold feet. I wasn't worried about meeting Connie again; she'd asked me to come, after all, and she'd never been very intimidating anyway. But the others . . . they'd all be gathered at the funeral tomorrow, certainly; hardly the place or the circumstance for a family reunion. Michelle and Rob Kurland and their remaining son Joel, Annette and Dr. Tom Henry, Congressman Uncle Oscar Ferguson and Aunt Elinor—they'd all be there. My choosing to live my life apart from them . . . well, they were bound to feel insulted. I'd worried about that before, but not a whole lot since we were separated by geography as well as by lack of fellow feeling. But now we'd all be there together, at Raymond's funeral, and they were sure to resent me. They'd see me as rejecting everything they had to offer in favor of what to them was nothing more than petty pursuits. They wouldn't be human if they weren't offended.

And suddenly I didn't want to offend them, I didn't want them to resent me. The Deckers were the only relatives I had, even if they were relatives-by-marriage only. My own people were dead, and I was reasonably sure I didn't have any unknown distant cousins floating around somewhere in the world. I was astonished at this sudden longing for *family* that came over me. For the very first time, I questioned the wisdom of having broken away from the Deckers.

The cab was taking me to Mt. Vernon Street on Beacon Hill, to the house where Raymond and the twins and Stuart had all spent their childhoods. The house had been built by their great-grandfather, and to the subsequent generations it remained the family homestead. Raymond had moved back in when his parents died; by then he had a wife and a child to move in with him. The others in the family maintained homes in Brookline and Dover and other places nearby, no one ever really straying far. The Mt. Vernon Street house was one of the few free-standing buildings on Beacon Hill, two or three times as wide as its neighbors. But I remembered Connie's once saying they really could use more room, considering the amount of entertaining she was expected to do. Raymond wouldn't hear of it; family tradition would be upheld come hell or high water.

Connie was waiting for me. Her appearance was appalling; it had been a long time since I'd seen her last, but it was more than the advance of age that had changed her so. Shadows under the eyes, creases down the cheeks, clenched jaw, eyes preternaturally bright. "Hello, Connie."

"Gillian? Oh, you've changed so much! I'm not sure I would have known you!" She practically pulled me in through the door, as though afraid I'd change my mind and go away again. Obeying orders, I left my suitcase in the hallway and followed her into the family room.

Connie hadn't stopped talking from the moment she'd opened the door. The gist of it was how glad she was I'd come and she didn't know what to do and she was about to go out of her mind. I resisted the urge to tell her to stop being melodramatic. That was uncharitable and, besides, perhaps she was none too stable at that; she was sounding less and less like the Connie I remembered. "Gillian, they just won't listen to me, none of them," she was saying. "They never did listen to me, but this time... this time it *matters*, don't you see?"

What I saw was an extremely distraught woman. What I had yet to see was if there was any realistic basis for her distraction. "Connie, try to calm yourself. This can't be good for you. Try taking deep breaths."

She did; it helped a little. "Oh, Gillian, I'm sorry. It's just that everything is so... I could do with a drink." She fixed us both one and then suddenly remembered her duties as a hostess. "Oh—are you hungry? Would you like something to eat?"

"I ate on the plane." I took a sip of the drink I didn't want and waited.

Now that she did have someone to listen to her, Connie didn't know what to say. I watched her struggling for words, and then without warning all of her nervous energy seemed to go out of her like air from a deflating balloon. She collapsed onto a sofa, slopping a little of her drink over her hand. "I know how this must look. The shallow wife unable to cope without a husband to lean on. That's what they all think." She sounded bitter. "But it's not that! It's not that at all. Somebody hates us, Gillian! Somebody's out to kill us all!''

This was worse than I thought. There was a stack of crystal coasters on the table beside the sofa; I took Connie's drink as well as my own and put them down. I sat next to her and put my arm around her shoulders. "Connie. Do you know how *that* sounds?"

"Paranoid, no doubt. Oh, Gillian, I wish Raymond were here! I miss him so."

Of course she did. I knew the feeling well; I'd been through it myself, that debilitating loss of your life's partner. There's nothing else quite like it in the world.

It's never easy losing a spouse, but Raymond's death would leave a gap in more than just his wife's life. He'd be missed by all of them, intensely so. Raymond had been the cornerstone of the Decker family—its driving energy, its directionsetter, its final arbiter of disputes. As for myself, I'd not seen him in ten years, and I wished—too late—that I'd not waited so long to come back.

After a time Connie had regained enough control that she could talk rationally. "I've been thinking about it, and I've come to the conclusion that what happened to Theo is not connected to what's happening now. That was an isolated...incident." Her face crumpled; she'd probably never before spoken of her son's death as an *incident*, a trivializing word for what must have been the biggest trauma of her life until now. "Those kidnappers...they just wanted money. They were vicious and sadistic—" She broke off suddenly, shaking her head; she couldn't stand to think about that. "But this time," she went on in agitation, "this time there've been no demands for ransom or anything like that. There's just somebody out there who's killing us off, one at a time. Somebody hates us."

"Can you bear to talk about the kids?" I asked her. "Were they together when they died?"

"No, they all died separately. And each time they were away from home for the weekend. So they could be got at, you see."

Young Bobby Kurland had been the first to die. He'd gone with friends for a ski weekend at Stowe, in February, braving sub-zero temperatures for the joy of sliding down a mountain on two fiberglass slats strapped to his feet. Their first day there, it had happened. Bobby had started down a long slope but never made it to the bottom. They found him smashed into a tree, the front of his skull crushed. And they found something else, as well: boot prints in the snow, leading to the tree and then away again. Someone had found Bobby and had *not* gone for help, a turn of the screw the family could have done without.

But Connie construed it differently. "It was the killer, you see," she explained with every semblance of reasonableness. "He was waiting for Bobby. To ambush him."

I didn't try to talk her out of it; best wait to hear the whole story. Ike Henry was next, Connie told me. He'd been attending a science fair in Toronto along with some of his classmates from Exeter. They were leaving the exhibition hall when a car came roaring down the street, lunging from side to side and clearly out of control. The teacher who'd taken the kids to the fair had watched in horror as Ike was pinned against a stone wall with a force that all but cut his body in two. The driver had backed off from the wall and driven away before any of the onlookers could recover from their shock. That sent a chill down my spine; Stuart had also died in a hit-and-run accident. But the driver of the car that killed Ike had never been found, a fact that Connie, never too strong on cause and effect, interpreted to mean the killing was deliberate.

Lynn Ferguson's death was the strangest of all. At seventeen, Lynn had turned into an expert swimmer; she'd won a number of local and state championships and was trying to make the Olympics team. The feeling in the family was that she had a good chance of succeeding. So in April Lynn had gone to New York for a swimming meet, an early Olympics trials competition that she'd been training for for almost a year. She'd won her first heat and gone back to the hotel to change for dinner. When she didn't show up to meet her teammates in the lobby, her coach went up to check on her. Lynn, the championship swimmer, had drowned—in her hotel bathtub. The soap she'd slipped on was there, and the blood-covered water spigot matched exactly the indentation in her temple where she'd hit. The medical examiner said Lynn had never regained consciousness, and therefore she'd drowned in the bathwater.

Connie covered her face with her hands. "Those kids never took baths," she said in a muffled voice. "They always took showers. Theo too." She dropped her hands into her lap. "I doubt if Lynn had had a bath since she was old enough to work the shower controls.''

That seemed pretty flimsy evidence. ''You can't be sure of that.''

Connie sighed. ''Yes, I'm sure. I asked Elinor.''

Well, Lynn's mother should know, if anyone would. But still . . .

''Then this month—Raymond. Burned to death. And everyone's accepting that stupid story that he fell asleep smoking. Raymond always said I ought to have at least one smoke-free room wherever we were. He never even smoked in hotel bedrooms. If we didn't have a suite, he'd go into the bathroom to light up. Raymond did *not* start that fire!'' She took a deep breath. ''Look at the pattern, Gillian. Bobby in February. Ike in March. Lynn in April. Raymond in May. One a month. Like clockwork.''

And June was just a week away. ''Is that what you're afraid of? That you'll be next? You think you're in danger?''

''I'd have to be an idiot *not* to think it! We're all in danger—but I can't make anyone see that.'' Her eyes suddenly grew wide. ''And now you're in danger too! You're a Decker—oh, Gillian! I shouldn't have asked you to come here! Oh, my! What have I done?''

Whew. I knew what conventional wisdom required of me; I was suppose to pooh-pooh her fears— nicely—and try to reassure her, to persuade her that her suspicions were groundless. The four deaths in the family, I should say, were nothing more than what they appeared to be: accidents. But I couldn't do that. Because at least part of what she was saying made a

chilling sort of sense. I wasn't convinced that someone was out to kill off the entire Decker clan, but four
violent deaths in a row...how could anyone dismiss
that as mere coincidence? And one a month? Like a
schedule? "Why weren't you at the Martha's Vineyard house with Raymond?" I asked Connie.

"I was going down the next day. I had some errands to take care of here first. Oh, if I'd only let the
errands go and gone with him..."

Then maybe she could have gotten him out of the
house in time. "Was the whole house destroyed?"

"No, only that one wing. That's one of the reasons
they think Raymond caused it, because it was local-
ized." She looked at me hopelessly. "You probably
think I'm crazy too."

"No, Connie. I don't think you're crazy at all."

Hope returned. "You believe me?"

"Well...I'm not sure. Do the, er, police suspect
anything?"

"Which police? The ones in Vermont? Canada?
New York? Martha's Vineyard? They all died in different places. I did tell the man who investigated Raymond's death what I thought." She smiled wryly. "He
listened very politely."

Hm. I didn't want to think that one person was
responsible for all four deaths, but there was one
connection—possibly a coincidence—that Connie
obviously wasn't letting herself think about. And that
was the nature of the deaths. They all four involved
mutilations of some sort. Bobby Kurland and Lynn
Ferguson had had their skulls smashed. Ike Henry had
been cut almost in two. And Raymond Decker had

burned to death. No quick easy bullet through the brain for any of them. If Raymond and the three kids had indeed been murdered, then it was by someone who wanted to make their deaths as grim and as hurtful as possible. Someone filled with hate.

The phone rang. Connie looked at me helplessly. "Would you, Gillian? I don't want to talk to anybody tonight."

That sounded more like the Connie I remembered. I didn't want to talk to anyone either, since whoever was calling was bound to be a Decker and I needed time to think over what Connie had told me. Besides, it had been ten years since I'd walked out and I had no right to expect a friendly reception.

Sure enough, it was a Decker—Annette Decker Kurland, twin *extraordinaire*. I swallowed and in an unsteady voice identified myself. There was a long, tense pause at the other end of the line. But then Annette recovered and thanked me for coming, even managing to inject some warmth into her voice. "Are you staying with Connie?" she wanted to know.

"Yes, I plan to."

"Good. She needs someone with her, but she doesn't seem to want any of us there." Annette's voice was deep, and she spoke in a deliberate manner, like someone who never allowed herself to be rushed. "Connie's been . . . distraught."

"I know."

"She's there in the room with you? Listening?"

"That's right, Annette. I learned only today about Ike. I am so sorry—what a waste! I can't tell you how sorry I am."

"Thank you. And you're right, it is a waste. A stupid waste of a young life. I don't know if I'll ever get over it, to tell you the truth. In a way, losing a child is even worse than losing a husband . . . oh dear, I didn't mean it's easier on Connie than it was on me. Don't tell her I said that."

"I won't."

Then she said something odd: "Besides, Raymond was my brother. I knew him a lot longer than Connie did." That sounded as if she thought the family tragedies *had* been harder on her than on Connie. Too many deaths, too close together; nobody was thinking straight. Annette said, "Gillian, if Connie brings up the detective again, try to talk her out of it? Please?"

Detective? "I'll do my best." That seemed a safe thing to say. What detective?

"The funeral's at eleven," Annette went on. "I'll pick you both up at ten-thirty. I don't want Connie going alone," she emphasized. "There'll be reporters, unfortunately, and she's not up to coping with that hassle."

"Reporters," I repeated, and heard Connie groan. "I hadn't thought of that. All right, Annette, we'll be ready at ten-thirty."

"Gillian," she said quietly, "I'm glad you're back."

I was pleased; she sounded as if she meant it. I hung up and turned to Connie, wondering whether to ask her about the detective or not.

But she didn't give me a chance. "Reporters!" she exploded. "They have no respect for anyone's private grief! They've been all over the place, shouting questions and trying to get at you when you go from the house to the car! They just won't leave you alone!''

"I didn't see anyone outside when I got here."

"Because Uncle Oscar pulled some strings to make them ease up. But they'll try to get into the funeral, the twins say. Rob's had to hire guards to keep them out of the cemetery tomorrow. Gillian, you should see some of the things they've written! Somebody sent me a newspaper that said 'A Family Marked for Tragedy' right on the front page! *The front page*!''

That must have galled them all; the Deckers had a near-obsessive distaste for publicity about their private lives. They avoided it like poison. "Tell me about the detective."

"The . . . oh. I wanted to hire one, to investigate everything, starting with Bobby's so-called accident on the ski slope. But Annette and Michelle pointed out that *we* were the ones who'd end up being investigated, if the detective had to look for things in Raymond's and the kids' lives that might have led to their being murdered. And they were right. It was a dumb idea.''

Not so dumb, if the four deaths truly were the result of murderous intent on the part of person or persons unknown. But the twins had a point; the detective would have to concentrate on the family. If the killer was indeed some unknown maniac, as seemed likely, then any such professional investigation of the family would not only be pointless but most probably hurtful as well. I don't think Connie understood what a thorough investigation would entail; she'd have to talk not only about Raymond but about Theo as well. A little earlier she'd barely been able to say his name without choking.

Connie and I talked on for a couple of hours, until we were both drooping with exhaustion. Connie'd talk a little, then cry a little, and then she'd ask me questions about my life without listening to the answers. The conversation never strayed far from the four deaths in the family; Connie kept coming back to them no matter what we were talking about. She had nothing more to add to what she'd said before, but she kept repeating it over and over. It had become a compulsion with her, this need to talk about murder.

I didn't know how much of what she was saying I could trust. But regardless of the interpretation Connie put on events, four of our people did die violently; there was no disputing that. If only the authorities were as concerned as the news reporters were! I couldn't believe the police were as indifferent as Connie made them out to be; she didn't always know everything that was going on. I'd have to ask one of the others tomorrow.

Tomorrow. A day I'd like to excise from the calendar. I'd come here thinking I'd be attending one funeral when in effect it would be the same as four. Bobby, Lynn, and Ike—I'd never had a chance to mourn their deaths. And now Raymond's name had been added to the list. The thought of *all* of them dead was just too much to cope with.

I asked Connie to show me to my room. I needed to take a sleeping pill and blot it all out for a while.

THREE

On the morning of the funeral, Connie Decker had already gone into her vague-and-distant mode by the time I got down to breakfast. She was there but not there, present in body but not in spirit. She didn't want to talk about anything to do with the funeral, nothing at all. I didn't push her; this was Connie's notion of self-control, her way of bracing herself for the ordeal to come. Besides, the glazed look in her eyes suggested she'd taken something to calm her down.

The family had decided on a brief ceremony to be held in a private cemetery—no church, no funeral home, and an Episcopalian minister who'd do no more than lead a prayer at the end. The twins, Rob Kurland, and Oscar Ferguson would speak at the gravesite. While that was going on, a team of caterers would move into Connie's house and prepare a buffet for the callers who would be stopping by later. Connie was nervous about that part; her housekeeper didn't like having caterers around. The twins had arranged it.

For some reason I couldn't get warm. I woke up chilled to the bone and was still feeling the occasional shudder when Annette Henry came by to pick us up. I was nervous about this first meeting and stood watching through a window as a chauffeur opened the door of a gray Rolls to let out a tall woman dressed in black, the top half of her face hidden by the brim of the hat she was wearing. She seemed to be alone. "Where's Tom?" I asked Connie.

"Oh, didn't I tell you?" she answered absently. "They're getting a divorce."

A *divorce*. So Annette had to contend with the collapse of a marriage on top of everything else...I fought down another shudder and composed myself the best I could to greet my sister-in-law. When she came in, she first murmured something to Connie and then turned to me.

I was looking at an impeccably groomed woman who was even more attractive now than she'd been ten years ago. Annette and her twin sister both had immense presence; they would have been dynamite on a theater stage. Just by walking into the house on Mt. Vernon Street, Annette had taken charge of it. Her eyes had deep shadows under them and her face wore the same pinched look as Connie's; but where Connie seemed on the edge of succumbing to hysteria or depression or worse, Annette was still in control. Four family deaths in quick succession were enough to make anyone a little nuts—anyone except a Decker born and bred.

Annette took my hands and said, "I always thought you'd come back." She spoke with the same cool deliberation she'd used on the telephone the night before. "I'm only sorry it has to be under these circumstances."

"So am I," I answered sincerely, strangely grateful for her...forgiveness? For her understanding. "I'd have come earlier if I'd known about Ike and the other two."

"Ike's dead. Nothing can be done about that now." She forced a little smile and said, "I'm glad to see you again, Gillian. You're looking good. Where are you living now?"

I told her where I was living and what I was doing there; it didn't take long to bring her up to date. "You really didn't know where I was?"

She raised an elegant eyebrow. "You didn't exactly keep us informed."

"I realize that, but you...have ways of finding things out, don't you? All of you. Somehow I thought you always knew where I was and what I was doing."

That brought a slight smile. "Oh, dear. You make us sound like the FBI. We did follow your career the first few years after you left, while you were still in New York. But then we lost track of you."

Then they stopped bothering, she meant. "Well," I said, at a loss.

After an awkward moment, we both decided it was time to go. Connie was ready and waiting for us.

When we went to get into the car, two men with cameras swooped down on us, clicking away. I followed Annette's lead and ignored them. But as soon as the chauffeur closed the door behind us, Connie burst out, "I thought Uncle Oscar had put a stop to that!"

Annette spoke soothingly. "All Oscar can do is apply a little pressure to the newspaper owners. At least there's no TV camera crew here shoving microphones in our faces. I hate that."

Even though it had been ten years since I last saw either of the women I was riding with, the drive to the private cemetery was mostly a silent one. That was no time for chatting. Besides, it was Raymond I was thinking of then, of the horrible way he'd died and of what his loss would mean to the family. Connie was fighting tears, none too successfully. Last night I'd asked if she had a recent picture of him; the photo she handed me showed a man who'd settled comfortably into his middle years. Raymond's black hair had started to gray, and the laugh lines around his mouth were more pronounced than I remembered them. There was no sag under the chin, though; the Decker jaw was as firm as ever. One corner of Raymond's mouth was lifted, as if he were amused. He'd been a good-looking man.

There were more reporters waiting at the cemetery entrance, and this time TV cameras as well. The windows of the Rolls were up, but that didn't stop the newspeople from shouting their questions at us as we drove by. Most of what they said was unintelligible through the glass, but one of them I heard quite clearly; she wanted to know who I was. I couldn't believe they were making this much fuss over the death of one lone financier, even if his last name was Decker. Raymond had been an important man, but he'd kept out of the public eye; most of the world didn't even know he existed. No, it had to be the circumstances of his death that drew them, the fact that he was the fourth member of the same family to die in as many months. Those seekers-after-truth with their cameras and their tape recorders were hoping for a nice juicy

murder story to take back to their editors. The cemetery gates closed behind us, with the guards Rob Kurland had hired glowering at the crowd outside.

Five rows of folding chairs had been set up along
one side of the grave for the family; I hesitated when
I saw how many people there were. Everybody in the
western hemisphere who'd been born a Decker, married to a Decker, or descended from a Decker was
there. And then I was in the midst of them, all those
faces I hadn't seen for so long. I heard more *Hello,
Gillians* and *Thank you for comings* than I could respond to. None of them seemed surprised to see me;
Annette had wasted no time in spreading the word.

And none of them seemed particularly glad to see
me, either, truth to tell; I hoped that was because we
were at Raymond's funeral and not because they'd
have preferred me to stay lost. There were some faces
there I didn't know, or only vaguely remembered,
from other branches of the family. At the last minute
we were joined by a sandy-haired man of somewhat
shorter stature than the Deckers—Dr. Tom Henry,
Annette's soon-to-be ex-husband. I was seated in the
last row next to the young Joel Kurland. I shivered,
from the cold; Joel gave me a sad little smile and
turned his attention to the funeral.

The arrival of Raymond's widow was the signal for
the ceremonies to begin; Connie kept her eyes on her
hands in her lap and wouldn't look at anybody. The
first to speak was Oscar Ferguson.

The Congressman from Massachusetts had an appearance that suited his role; he was tall, solidly built,
and had a full head of beautiful gray hair—*très dis-*

tingué without making a joke of it. The only thing that had changed about Uncle Oscar in the past decade was that he'd grown a tad jowly. But even that was right, in a way; if he were too pretty in his late middle age, the voters might stop trusting him. But Oscar's true gift was his indisputable ability as a speaker; he had a Richard-Burton-sober voice and he knew how to use it.

"I've lost a nephew," he started out, "but Raymond Decker was more than just one man's nephew. He was a man who changed the world he found himself in, and he left it better than he found it." That rich actory voice rolled on, extolling Raymond's virtues as far-sighted businessman, philanthropist, lover of his country and devotee of the arts (*devotee of the arts*?), sportsman, world traveler, concerned citizen, and lodge brother. "But more than anything else," Oscar said, "Raymond Decker was a family man. He knew that the family is the basis on which this country is built, the bedrock on which all individual achievement rests." That part sounded like a few political speeches I'd heard Uncle Oscar make. He went on, "Our family is less, now that Raymond is gone. But the bedrock remains. Raymond managed to strengthen even that. We will never see another man quite like Raymond Decker. I mourn his passing."

Then, to my surprise, he sat down; I'd expected a much longer peroration. But immediately Michelle Kurland was on her feet and speaking. I knew it was Michelle, because her clothes were different from those worn by the woman I'd ridden with to the cemetery.

She was every bit as stunning-looking as her twin. They must be forty-four, forty-five by now; I hoped I looked that good in another seven or eight years. Hell, I'd settle for looking that good *now*. Michelle was saying about the same things Oscar Ferguson had said, but she was adding a few personal reminiscences of her brother. She articulated each word carefully, making sure she was understood.

From where I was sitting I could barely see the side of Rob Kurland's face as he listened attentively to what his wife was saying; his expression was unreadable. I had a good view of Tom Henry's face, though, Annette's husband; he looked miserable. Aunt Elinor sat next to Connie, leaning toward her protectively but saying nothing; I could see only the backs of their heads.

On the other side of the grave stood a group of mourners, all strangers to me. Most of them kept their eyes on the casket poised over the open grave; all of them looked properly somber. Michelle finished speaking and Annette took her place at the head of the grave. Like the two speakers before her, Annette stressed Raymond's belief in family as the single most important thing in human existence. They were all saying the same things, but they were pretty good at finding different ways to say them.

Then Rob Kurland stood up to speak. "He was my brother-in-law, he was my business partner, he was my friend," he began in a raspy voice. "I shall miss all three of them." It was the first good look at Rob I'd had, and I was shocked by his appearance. He'd always been thin, but now he was almost cadaverous-looking. The bones in his face were too prominent; his skin was not a healthy color. I wanted to ask Joel sitting next to me if his father had been ill but decided I'd better wait.

Perspiration had begun to bead on Joel's forehead. The man sitting directly in front of me, one of the out-of-state Deckers, pulled out a handkerchief and mopped the back of his neck. The sun felt warm on the backs of my hands, but they were the only parts of my body that did feel warm. I just couldn't get rid of the chill I'd woken up with that morning.

I'd been under the impression that only family members were going to speak at Raymond's funeral, but such was not the case. As soon as Rob sat down, there began a parade of other speakers, Raymond's friends and business associates, a few local politicians. Fortunately, they all kept their speeches short; no one spoke more than three or four minutes. One man said the head of the Decker family had been a man of strength, dignity, and the highest ethical standards. I wondered if Raymond would have been embarrassed by that. Probably not; he'd had a way of letting hyperbole roll right off him.

The last eulogizer was the state's lieutenant-governor, I later found out. He said we'd lost a man who had demonstrated repeatedly in his life that the family was the bedrock on which this country rested; he must have used the same speechwriter as Uncle Oscar. Then the minister moved to the head of the grave and we were all on our feet. I didn't hear one word of the prayer the man uttered, and I wondered if anyone else did either; I for one was all too conscious of that casket waiting to be lowered into the ground. The minister finished; the casket was lowered; the funeral was over.

And everyone in the Decker family took off in a different direction.

I was left standing in front of my folding chair with my mouth open; even young Joel Kurland had bolted. The minister and the mourners on the other side of the grave were exchanging puzzled glances; they'd probably expected to move along a waiting line of Deckers while murmuring sympathetic words over and over again. But with everyone scattered like that . . .

Then they started coming back. Annette spoke to the minister; Oscar and Michelle moved among the mourners, accepting their condolences. They'd all just needed a moment alone, that was all. Eventually a sort of line did form, which I joined. But there was no eye contact among the Deckers, no sharing of grief; every Decker was isolated from every other Decker, each one an island of his or her own personal sorrow. After great pain, Emily Dickinson said, a formal feeling comes; the remoteness would disappear in time and there'd be a closing of ranks later. God, how I wished this day were over.

But we still had the postceremony gathering at the house to get through. This time I barely noticed the reporters at the cemetery gate because of something Connie had just said. "Those people on the other side of the grave," she ventured tentatively, "do you suppose it was one of them who killed Raymond?"

Annette made a sound of exasperation which she quickly suppressed. "*No*, Connie, none of those peoe would want to hurt Raymond. You really must put that idea out of your mind." All during the ride home Annette worked on her sister-in-law, reasoning with her and calming her, until she had Connie actually apologizing for her suspicions. What Annette didn't know was that I was harboring those same suspicions myself.

People like the Deckers are always objects of envy, and sometimes that envy can become obsessive and turn dangerous. The Deckers lived well, they were a prominent family, they *belonged*. Someone outside their circle of privilege could very easily be so soured with jealousy that he'd go right over the edge and start killing the symbols of what he couldn't have for himself. The Deckers knew that; they'd suffered from it once before, when someone had kidnapped Raymond and Connie's son Theo and ended up killing him even though the ransom had been paid. So there was just no way the rest of the Deckers could dismiss the four deaths in the family as coincidence, accidents, tragic bad luck. They had to be suspicious. They just weren't telling Connie.

That made a kind of sense. Connie wasn't a player; she was a passenger. When I'd known her earlier, she'd rarely made decisions on her own. She just went along with what the rest of the family decided. If Annette and the others thought some lunatic was stalking them, they'd take steps to protect themselves and Connie but try to shield her from the knowledge. Why frighten her? Talk her out of it, soothe her, make her think everything was all right. That wasn't the way I'd do it, but the Deckers would see it as guarding their weakest link.

There were a few cars parked near the family home on Mt. Vernon Street, the passengers courteously waiting until the new widow had returned. Once the various Deckers started coming inside, a lot of the remoteness that had been in evidence at the cemetery disappeared—because they were no longer on public display, I supposed.

Annette took off her wide-brimmed hat and gave me a surprise. Her black hair was cut short, almost as short as a brush cut. It was the sort of hairstyle that required no attention other than the occasional trim. Someone wearing that hairstyle was saying to the world, *Look, I have better things to do with my time than fuss over hair*. A busy-woman haircut. And it suited Annette to a *T*; she looked stunning. Michelle kept her hat on so I couldn't be sure, but it looked as if she might have the same cut as her twin.

Dr. Tom was there, his sandy curls more noticeable than ever among so many ebony-haired Deckers. He and Annette spoke briefly and then moved apart; I wondered how many of the out-of-towners knew they were divorcing. Tom was standing by the buffet, scowling at a plate of ham slices. I went over to talk to him.

"Ah, Gillian," he said when he saw me approaching. "What a sad homecoming for you."

I said I would have come earlier if I'd known about the other deaths in the family. Tom didn't look much better than Rob, but he was holding up about as well as could be expected of a man who'd lost a son, a nephew, a niece, and a brother-in-law all in a period of four months. I told him how sorry I was about Ike.

Then, oddly, he said the same thing Annette had said: "Ike's dead now. There's nothing we can do about that." He straightened his shoulders and changed the subject. "Are you going to Martha's Vineyard with Connie?"

"Oh, I don't think so. I'll have to get back to Chicago."

"Is that where you're living now? Are you still directing plays?"

I told him about the museum. "I'm going to stay with Connie a few more days—I don't think she should be alone with only the house staff for company. Just until the worst of it is over."

He nodded. "Yes, Connie needs people around her. All the time. It's going to take more than a few days for her to get over this."

I sighed. "I know."

"Can't your museum struggle on without you for a week or so?" Tom asked. "Come down to the Vineyard for a few days anyway—it'll give us a chance to get reacquainted."

"You're going down?" That surprised me, because of the divorce.

He nodded absently. "I need some time alone, to do some thinking—Annette's off to Paris in a few days."

And he was going to sit in that empty house, without his wife or his child...and think himself into a depression? He looked halfway there now. "Do you think that's a good idea?" I asked cautiously.

"It's necessary," he answered shortly. "These past few months have been torture. We could all do with an accident-free environment for a while."

I hesitated, and then took the plunge. "Connie thinks they weren't accidents."

Before he could answer, I felt a hand on my arm. It was Michelle, looking solicitous. "We're all concerned about Connie, Gillian," she said in the same deliberate speech that her twin used. "She's not very strong, and these fantasies she's having about murder are just making things worse. It would help if you didn't encourage her."

Hello, Michelle. "Of course. I understand. But Connie seems to be handling it fairly well."

She smiled, a little. "It's the tranquilizer that's doing the handling, I'm afraid."

"She's on tranquilizers? I wondered if she'd taken something."

"It's all right," Tom said. "I prescribed them."

Michelle said, "Gillian, we need to sit down and have a good long talk. So many years . . . we have a lot to catch up on. Why don't you come stay with us tonight?"

"But Connie—"

"Annette is staying with Connie tonight," Michelle interposed silkily. "She won't be alone, if that's what you're thinking about."

"Well, yes, that was—"

"Don't worry, Gillian. We're not going to leave her by herself."

"In that case, I'll be glad to come. Thank you."

Michelle murmured something and slipped away. "That was smooth," Tom said, one eyebrow cocked. "As usual."

I looked past his shoulder and saw Michelle whispering to her twin; Annette nodded once in response. "Yes, it was smooth," I replied. "They don't want to leave me alone with Connie."

Tom shot me a quick look. "You picked up on that, did you? Well, well. Does it begin to feel familiar?"

Being manipulated, he meant. And yes, it was beginning to feel familiar. I'd almost managed to forget how good the Deckers were at arranging everything exactly the way they wanted it.

Everything.

FOUR

THE KURLANDS lived in Sherborn, so for the second time that day I got into the back seat of someone else's car for a ride I didn't want to take. Michelle had tossed off her hat before climbing in—and yes, her hair had the same short crop as her twin's. Joel was quick to shed necktie and suit jacket before getting in the back with me. Michelle drove because Rob said his eyes were hurting; I asked if he'd been ill.

He swiveled around to look at me. "No," he answered in his raspy voice. "Why?"

I shrugged. "You look so thin, Rob."

He gave a mirthless laugh. "We've all lost weight these last few months. Even Joel." Of course they had; I should have known. I looked at the boy next to me.

He favored me with a lopsided grin. "You aren't going to start lecturing me on how I should eat more, are you, Aunt Gillian?"

"I wouldn't dream of it," I assured him earnestly.

"Fantastic!" he grinned. "Everybody else at the funeral did, all those out-of-state relatives. The Newport people were the worst, especially Aunt Elizabeth. Mom, is she really my aunt?"

"She's your great-aunt by marriage," Michelle said over her shoulder. "Elizabeth *is* a bit of a fussbudget, but she was just concerned about you."

"Yeah, I know. Well, it's all over now, so everybody'll start eating again anyway."

"Joel," his mother and father said together. He fell silent.

Uh-oh—why did they shut him up? What had Joel been on the brink of saying that his parents didn't want me to hear? I tried to meet Michelle's eyes in the rearview mirror but she wouldn't look up.

When the last of the postfuneral callers had left the house on Mt. Vernon Street, I'd gone to tell Connie I'd be staying with the Kurlands that night. She already knew; Annette had explained. For a woman who less than twenty-four hours earlier had been frantic for me to come to Boston, Connie now seemed remarkably indifferent as to whether I went or stayed. Maybe it was Raymond's funeral, or maybe it was the tranquilizers. Or maybe the twins had been working on her.

Connie really needed to get away from that house for a while, but I didn't know that Martha's Vineyard was any better—where her husband had died, and only recently; that place would have as many memories as the Mt. Vernon Street house. I said to Michelle and Rob that a trip to some place like Montego Bay or Hawaii might be good for Connie. Michelle replied she'd already made such a suggestion but Connie hadn't been too enthusiastic about the idea. Rob said they'd try it again later, when Connie was feeling a little better.

They could probably talk her into it, if they put their minds to it; Connie was very suggestible. But in the meantime, it looked as if Martha's Vineyard offered the best temporary retreat. I thought of Tom Henry standing by the buffet table, urging me to go down to the island. I halfway wanted to go.

I had a house on Martha's Vineyard. It had been Stuart's, the newest and smallest of the various Decker households there. When I left ten years ago, I told the twins to feel free to use it as a guest house or in any other way they wanted; that was what had finally convinced them I was leaving for good. In ten years I'd never once received a maintenance bill or a tax notice, not even during the years when the Deckers knew where I was. But the house would be ready for occupancy tomorrow if I wanted it; it was a Decker house, after all, and the Deckers took care of their own.

Brighton, Newton, Wellesley—eventually we reached Sherborn. The minute the car pulled into the garage of a big house surrounded by woods, Joel was out of the car and heading indoors before he remembered his manners and came back for my suitcase. "Which room, Mom?"

"The one next to yours." Michelle said we might as well get me settled first, so we followed Joel inside and up the stairs to the second floor. He deposited my suitcase in one room and disappeared into the next. Across the hall was another boy's bedroom; I glanced in and looked away quickly.

Michelle noticed. "Yes, that's Bobby's room. Neither Rob nor I have felt up to packing away his things. But I think I can do it now."

Why now? I didn't ask.

My room was spacious and comfortable and had a frequently used look to it. Michelle watched me unpack. "Is that all you brought? Aren't you staying?"

"I have obligations in Chicago," I reminded her.

"I know, but I thought you'd stay a little while, at least. Come down to Martha's Vineyard with us, Gillian. You can take a week or two, can't you?"

As a matter of fact, I could; there was nothing urgent demanding my presence in Chicago. And I did want answers about what had been happening to my relatives. "I'll call my assistant later," I temporized. "Perhaps something can be worked out."

She gave my hand a squeeze. "Good. You *should* stay. You walked out of our lives . . . how long ago?"

"Almost ten years."

"Ten years! It's been that long, has it. For ten years we don't hear a word from you, and now you want to leave again so soon? Well, I won't hear of it. You get that assistant of yours on the phone and tell her . . . her?"

"Him."

"Tell him to start *assisting*, because you're going to be busy getting acquainted with your family again. Oh, Gillian, I *am* glad to see you. Don't run away this time!"

She was so hostessy-earnest that I had to laugh. "All right, I'll stay a while." It was hard to say no to either of the twins. Michelle stood staring out a window while I took some things into the bathroom. When I came back, she was still standing there, motionless, the late afternoon sun highlighting her profile, her clear-cut features framed tidily by the short-cut black hair. She looked…serene. At a time like this, she looked serene.

"I was sorry to hear Annette and Tom are divorcing," I said—and wondered at what I'd just done, choosing that particular moment to introduce so unpleasant a subject. Because I wanted to see that serenity disturbed? A mean-spirited thing to do. Small.

But Michelle took it in stride; Michelle took everything in stride. She waved a hand dismissively, not wanting to talk about it, and assumed what I recognized from ten years ago as the twins' favorite pose: left hand on left hip, right foot forward a little, nose tilted heavenward. She said, "Once Ike was gone, a lot of things were said that shouldn't have been said."

Between Annette and Tom, she meant. "That's unfortunate."

"Yes."

"Well, I hope Annette finds whatever it is she wants."

A shadow passed over Michelle's face. "What she wants is Ike back. The same way I want Bobby back."

Then Michelle began to talk of her dead son. It wasn't an emotional outpouring of long-bottled-up anguish, but rather a calm looking back over what Bobby had done, what he'd hoped to do, what he'd hoped to be. "He had a kind of self-knowledge that's rare in an eighteen-year-old," she said. "Bobby was confident but not headstrong. He wasn't afraid to make mistakes. He wasn't *afraid*, Gillian." She spoke of her son with love and pride; I wondered how long a period of mourning would be needed before she could speak of Raymond the same way.

I asked to see a picture. She brought me a framed eight-by-ten full-body shot of a young man in shorts and tennis shoes doing something with a rope on a sailboat. "Why, Michelle . . . he was a man!"

"Yes," she replied simply.

And an extraordinarily good-looking one at that. I could see nothing of the child Bobby that I knew in the muscular, competent-looking young man in the photograph. Could only one decade have made such a difference? Obviously, since I held the evidence in my hand. My heart went out to Michelle; to watch a child grow up strong and capable and then see him struck down when he's only beginning to realize his potential . . . "Bobby's death must be hard for Joel," I murmured. "I remember how close they were."

Her face lightened. "That's the strange thing, Gillian—Joel surprised us all. He all but worshiped Bobby, you know. Ever since Joel was old enough to walk, Bobby looked out for him . . . taught him things, showed him the ropes. But when his brother died, Joel didn't shut himself away in his room and wait to be comforted. *He* comforted *us*. I'm sorry he had to grow up so fast, but Joel's turned out to be a lot stronger than we thought."

"How old is he now?"

"Fifteen." She pressed her lips together. "It all comes down to Joel, now. He's our last hope."

Their hope for the future, for passing on the Decker genes and keeping the Decker family and business from vanishing into nothingness. A big burden for a fifteen-year-old.

After a few more minutes we went back downstairs. At the foot of the stairs, Rob was waiting with a cocktail shaker in his hands. "Gillian, I couldn't remember whether you liked martinis or not."

"Didn't then, do now."

"Ah. Well, have a seat and I'll bring you one."

Just then Joel came thundering down the stairs, dressed in jeans and a sweatshirt. "Hey, I'm going over to Mike's—okay?"

"*Hey*, okay," Rob said. "Back by six."

"Righty-o." Joel rushed out.

I looked at his parents. "Righty-o?"

Michelle smiled with mock resignation. "This year's fab phrase. Or is it a single word? Let's go in here."

I followed her into a room that had more windows than wall space, but the afternoon sun pouring in had a tinge of melancholy to it. I was seeing this house for the first time, since the Kurlands had bought it sometime after I'd left; they'd lived in Brookline before. I could hear the engine of something smaller than a car starting outside and roaring away. Rob came in carrying three martinis; we each took one and found seats. "Would you like something to nibble on?" he asked in his raspy voice.

"No, thanks. But there *is* something I would like. An explanation."

Rob stretched his long legs out in front of him, crossed his feet at the ankles. "Oh? Of what?"

"Of why you didn't want me to stay with Connie tonight."

He and Michelle exchanged a brief look, and then they both laughed. Michelle said, "I'd forgotten how direct you are, Gillian."

"Direct and persistent. Do I get an answer?"

"Of course you get an answer," she said. "We just wanted a chance to talk to you privately because we know what Connie must have been saying."

"She's been saying quite a lot."

"Tell us what?"

"Well, for one thing, she's saying that Raymond was murdered. And she thinks the three kids may have been too."

"Yes, she believes that."

"She also believes someone is out to kill off the entire Decker family. That is one frightened lady."

Michelle shook her head. "Poor Connie. I'd hoped she'd . . . well. This is what we were afraid would happen, when Annette told us you were back. You're just the person she'd pour it all out on. Part of the family and yet not part, if you don't mind my putting it that way."

I didn't.

Rob asked, "Did she tell you the whole thing? About the 'mysterious' footprints in the snow on the Vermont ski slope? And the hit-and-run driver in Toronto who was never caught? And the 'suspicious' bathtub accident in New York?"

"All that plus the fact that Raymond never smoked in bed," I added.

"Oh, yes—that too." Rob scowled. "Do you know she wanted to hire a private detective? We had a hell of a time talking her out of that."

"You think Connie's crazy," I said.

"No, of course we don't think Connie's crazy," he answered sharply, and then took a deep breath. He glanced at his wife. When she nodded, Rob told me heavily, "As a matter of fact, we think she's right. We think all four of them were murdered."

THEY HADN'T BEGUN to suspect anything until Ike Henry had been smashed against a wall in Toronto by a seemingly out-of-control automobile. Bobby's death they had sadly accepted as the skiing accident it appeared to be, and the footprints in the snow as those of someone who didn't want to get involved. But when less than a month later Bobby's cousin Ike also met with a violent death, they began voicing their first suspicions—tentatively, without conviction. Then when the following month Lynn Ferguson drowned in a hotel bathtub in New York, they were sure.

And "they" meant all of them: the Kurlands, the Henrys, and the Fergusons—everyone except Connie Decker. Connie didn't even start to find anything suspicious in the rash of family deaths until Raymond supposedly caused his own death with a lighted cigarette. But the others did, and had acted on it. They'd hired a bodyguard for Joel. They'd employed a firm of private detectives to investigate. And they'd made sure the police's efforts in Vermont, Canada, New York and Martha's Vineyard were all coordinated.

"So you see why we don't want Connie hiring a private detective," Michelle explained. "We didn't want her detective muddying the waters for *our* detectives."

That made sense, but... "But why didn't you just tell her so?"

Michelle exchanged a regretful look with Rob, who said, "We probably should have. But Connie never even thought of it until Raymond died, and then she kind of went off the deep end."

"It's hard to explain," Michelle said. "This all just happened a few days ago, you know, and Connie really went to pieces when the police said it looked as if Raymond had been smoking in bed. She was crying and screaming and talking like a wild woman... Connie's always been so placid, we didn't know what to make of it. It just seemed that the wisest thing to do was calm her down. Tom gave her a sedative, but she can't stay doped up all the time. When she's lucid, all her fears come rushing back in again."

I remembered the contrast between last night's frenzy and this morning's remoteness. "She took something before the funeral."

"Probably a double dose," Rob muttered.

"You're going to have to tell her," I persisted.

They both nodded. "The problem is finding the right time," Michelle said. "We're afraid that right now...well, it might push her over the edge. We'll give her a few more days."

If it had been anyone other than Connie they were talking about, I'd have found their attitude patronizing. But of all the people I knew, Connie Decker was undoubtedly the most poorly equipped to deal with serious trouble. It was the one thing about Raymond Decker that had always puzzled me, why he should have chosen so passive a wife. Raymond didn't need a woman he could dominate; he had no need to prove he was king of the hill. But theirs had been a comfortable marriage, as far as I could tell; evidently each one supplied the other with whatever was needed.

But that was in the past; now that ugly word *murder* was out in the open, or the semi-open. "Do you also agree with Connie that someone is out to kill off all the Deckers?" I asked the Kurlands.

Rob said, "We think it's a possibility. Someone who has a grudge against the family."

"Any idea who that might be?"

He shrugged. "Business enemy, perhaps? We've made a few. What gets me is the cowardliness of going after the children first."

"He skipped Joel," I said.

"Maybe he couldn't get to him, for some reason. But he, whoever he is, is starting after the adults now. Fooling the kids is one thing, but Raymond would have been on his guard. He was the first to suspect Bobby's accident was no accident. Yet the killer was able to get him just the same. We can't assume Joel is safe."

"Where's his bodyguard now?"

"We had to let him go," Michelle said tightly. "It wasn't working out—too many problems."

A chill ran down my back. "Yet you let him go to his friend's house alone."

Rob scowled. "We have to try for some degree of normalcy in our lives. Besides, our neighborhood employs a private security agency. No one comes in here that they don't know. You can be sure you got a good looking-over when we drove in."

"I didn't see anyone."

"That's the idea."

I got up and walked to the nearest window. "Lots of woods out there."

"All enclosed within an electric fence. Joel is about as safe here as he'd be anywhere. Remember, Bobby and the other two were away from home when they were killed."

That was true; it made a difference, I supposed. "Have your detectives found anything?"

"Nothing. Not a damned thing. The trail was pretty cold by the time they started investigating Bobby's death. But with Raymond, they have a better chance."

The phone rang, in another room. "Your turn," Michelle said. Rob groaned and got up and left. "I'm surprised it hasn't rung before now."

"Lots of phone calls?"

"Tons of them. And we can't just ignore them or let the answering machine take them. Business goes on."

"I can see why you want to get away for a while. I don't suppose Connie is any too eager to go to Martha's Vineyard, is she?"

"Connie swears she'll never set foot on that island again. But she'll change her mind, in time. However, we do want to make sure all evidence of the fire is removed before she goes. We have people working on it now."

"Tom Henry's going to the Vineyard. He says Annette is leaving for Paris in a few days."

"Yes, she's only just decided to go."

I didn't understand why Tom wanted to spend time with his in-laws during his divorce proceedings, but that was his business. Maybe it was the place that drew him, not the people; he could shut himself away in the house he'd shared with Annette for so many years and not see any of us. Them.

Just then Rob came back in. "That was the head of another outfit Raymond was thinking of seeding," he reported, and nodded as Michelle *oh-deared*. To me he said, "Raymond handled all the heavy-industry investing we did. Everyone he's been checking out has called in to see if his death will affect their chances of getting seed money from us. I've had to tell them yes, it will."

Rob and the twins would not be advertising for a replacement for Raymond; any new partner in the firm would have to be a Decker or married to one. They might consider bringing in one of the Rhode Island Deckers; but from what I remembered of that branch of the family, those Deckers were all pretty well settled in businesses of their own. And none of the immediate family could do the work; Tom Henry was a cardiac surgeon, Oscar Ferguson had a job in Washington, Elinor Ferguson ran the family's philanthropic foundation, and Joel Kurland was only fifteen. So, no replacement, at least not until Joel had finished Harvard Business School.

"We're going to have to go through his files," Michelle said with an air of soldiering-through. "He could have been close to a decision on some of them. It'd be a shame to miss out on a good investment only because it's in Raymond's area of expertise."

"Yes, I suppose." Rob sounded about as enthusiastic as she did. They both fell silent.

All of a sudden I was hit by a bad attack of cabin fever. "I want to go outside for a while—I need to think."

Michelle came over and gave me a restrained little hug. "You've had a lot thrown at you in the last twenty-four hours, haven't you? I'm sorry, Gillian. I wish you could have been spared all this."

So did I. I said I wouldn't be long and left through double doors that opened out to a patio. Through a break in the wooded area behind the house I caught a glimpse of another house, some distance away. I headed in the opposite direction.

A path wound through the trees; I wouldn't be going far, since I wasn't wearing the right kind of shoes for a lengthy stroll through the woods. The ground under my feet was crackly with twigs, leaf litter, and the occasional acorn the neighborhood squirrels had missed last autumn. But the trees had sprouted new leaves, and little green things were pushing their way up through the litter of the woodland floor. It was still early enough in the year that the flying pests that detract so considerably from sylvan charm everywhere were not yet in evidence. The woods were silent, so silent that the sound of my passage became an intrusion.

I found a tree stump to sit on. Michelle and the others had had time to adjust, to a degree, to the fact that someone wanted them dead; but I'd had less than a day to get used to the idea. There was one part of my mind that resisted the notion that the Deckers were being stalked by a killer, and the reason for that resistance was the most unrealistic imaginable. I simply could not bring myself to think of the Deckers as victims.

But plainly they were; first the kids, and now Raymond. Three well-loved children and the king of the clan—all of them gone. Of all the adults in the Decker family other than Stuart, I'd liked Raymond the most. The man had had style. When his father died, Raymond had accepted his new role of *paterfamilias* with grace and authority, Stuart had told me, making the transition as easy as possible for everyone concerned. I could believe it. Raymond was a man who found immense satisfaction in making things work, whether it was a big business deal or a small family outing. And he did it all without acting superior, without puffing himself up; I got a charge out of watching someone who was so thoroughly and yet so unostentatiously in control of his world as Raymond Decker had been.

With the twins, I was never quite that comfortable. Superwomen make me uneasy. Michelle and Annette both managed big careers and big family life with an ease that was almost insulting. In addition, they were exquisitely dressed at all times; no old clothes hung in *their* closets. They carried it all off with an insouciance that seemed to imply anyone could do it with a little foresight and planning—thus setting a standard impossibly out of reach for us lesser mortals. The twins were never anything but hospitable and cordial to me, but we just weren't on the same wavelength. They made me nervous.

Tom, I never got to know very well; his surgical skills were much in demand and he was forever flying off to one place or another to perform difficult operations. Rob, on the other hand, I had come to think of as a third twin; that's how well he fit into Decker life. He could have been born a Decker instead of simply being married to one. Connie too, I supposed; I couldn't imagine her living any life other than a Decker-surrounded one, going along amiably with whatever the more forceful family members decided. That was a strange time in my life, ten years ago; I couldn't be a Rob Kurland and I didn't want to be a Connie Decker, so I'd fled to more familiar stamping grounds in the hope of finding myself a warm spot there. I just couldn't see any place for myself in the Decker family.

Out loud, I said, "I ran away because I couldn't keep up with them." That was the first time I'd ever admitted that. It didn't make me feel any better.

So there I was, sitting on a tree stump in a Massachusetts woods, wearing the wrong shoes and feeling sorry for myself. With all the grief the Deckers had, I was feeling sorry for *myself*. That didn't make me feel better either. It dawned on me that all this monumentally unhelpful self-exploration was in fact only a diversionary tactic, a way of avoiding facing up to what was going on here.

The truth was, I was terrified. In all my life, I had never before known anyone who'd been *murdered*. My god, that was something you read about in the newspapers! And then I find that four of my late husband's family have all been murdered, and most likely the killing wasn't over yet. As much trouble as I had believing something this messy and out of control could be happening to the Deckers, I was still afraid.

Because *something* was happening—I didn't know who was behind it or why, or what would happen next; was I in danger? Connie had said as much after she'd pulled me here from Chicago. Because my name had once been Decker, was I now a target? I wanted to go home—I wanted to go back to my house and my museum and *my* life; I wanted it so much it hurt.

In short: I wanted to run away again.

I sat on that damned tree stump until my bottom turned numb. The sun was almost gone and the air was getting chilly; I hugged myself and stood up to pick my way among the leaf litter back toward the direction I'd come from. I really should have brought different shoes.

Things couldn't go on in this kind of limbo I'd created for myself and the Deckers; some sort of equilibrium had to be established. I went into the house and told Rob and Michelle that I'd stay with Connie until the repairs on her Martha's Vineyard house were completed, and then I'd take her there myself.

FIVE

THE NEXT DAY I went back to Connie's house on Mt.
Vernon Street, thinking Annette would be relieved to
be relieved. But she was in no hurry to go, perhaps
waiting for Tom to leave for Martha's Vineyard before returning to her own house in Brookline. At any
rate, it gave us a chance to talk, to try to reestablish a
kinship that had never been all that close to begin
with.

Connie was saying nothing about murder now. She
seemed more like the placid, accepting woman I'd always thought her to be, with one major exception: she
was unhappy. I'd never seen Connie unhappy before.
She'd always been a princessy sort of woman, leading
the kind of life in which tragedy simply didn't figure.
But after the double tragedy of seeing both her son
and her husband die violently, she'd had her break-
down and was now starting to show signs of being resigned to a life that had to look bleak and empty to
her. That surprising spurt of frenzy and accusation
that had brought me here was over. She'd stopped
fighting back.

I'd called my assistant in Chicago, explaining that
I'd be gone longer than I originally thought. He did a
poor job of concealing his pleasure; I could stay forever as far as he was concerned. Leonard had been
assistant curator of the museum longer than I had

been its curator; he'd thought, with some grounds, that he'd be promoted to the curatorship when my predecessor retired. When that didn't happen, he'd sort of gritted his teeth and hung on. Leonard never dragged his feet or worked against me; it's just that we weren't exactly buddies. He'd be in his element while I was away.

A few days passed, with all the family phoning or dropping in at least once a day to check on Connie. I had a long talk on the phone with Aunt Elinor in Georgetown; she told me she and Oscar would be going to Martha's Vineyard as soon as Congress recessed, in less than a week. A lot of Connie's friends came by, including the semi-anonymous Marcie who'd answered the phone when I'd first called from Chicago. I was impressed by the parade of well-wishers; how could so passive a person as Connie Decker have acquired so many concerned friends? Probably by never saying or doing anything that would offend anybody.

I asked Annette if she carried a picture of Ike. She did; I looked at a lean, black-haired youngster grinning confidently at the camera. Ike Henry had not been the grown man that Bobby Kurland was, but there were an alertness and a friendly curiosity in his face that were highly appealing. You could just see the intelligence in those eyes—and I found myself thinking, once again, *What a waste*.

"Tell me about him, Annette," I said.

She told me that Ike had been one of those people who could juggle a dozen different balls at once without dropping any. He'd been involved in a number of

school activities simultaneously without ever feeling
pressured; Ike simply didn't fail at what he tried. Annette had wanted him to go into the family business
but had raised no objection when he'd announced he
wanted to do medical research instead, because she'd
understood—they'd all understood—that Ike was
special. He'd already been accepted in Harvard's pre-
med program even though he still had one year to go
at Exeter. If there was a genius among the family's
younger generation, it was Ike. Annette told me this
without any false modesty or apology for what might
look like the hyperbole of maternal pride. It was simply a statement of fact: Ike was a genius.

So here was one more kid who'd been going to set
the world on fire—and he probably would have, too,
along with Bobby Kurland . . . and Lynn Ferguson? I
asked about her.

Annette tilted her head to one side, thinking.
"Connie ought to have a picture of Lynn—of all of
them." We went looking for Connie and found her in
the breakfast room pinching dead leaves off an Afri-
can violet. Annette asked her about photographs.
"Remember that picture Raymond took last summer
of all four of the kids—the one on the pier? You still
have a copy of that, don't you?"

Connie remembered. "I'm pretty sure Raymond
kept that one in his desk." She sniffed the fingers that
had been pinching the violet leaves. "How can anything that pretty smell so bad? Come on, let's go see."

We all trooped into Raymond's study, the first time
I'd been in there since I came back. Most of the furniture I remembered had been replaced with newer

pieces, but the wood paneling and the orderly book-shelves were the same. Connie rummaged through the desk drawers until she found what she was looking for. "Here it is. Gillian, why don't you keep this one? I can have another made. You should have a picture of your own."

What a sweet gesture. She handed me a five-by-seven glossy and stood next to me to look at it. Annette came up and looked over my other shoulder. We saw four healthy teenagers in swim suits standing on a wooden pier before a sea that glimmered with sun-light; the prow of some sort of boat was barely visible on the left. Lynn Ferguson was a coltish, long-legged adolescent, her skin bronze and her black hair shiny wet. Bobby Kurland's forearm rested easily on Ike Henry's shoulder, and Lynn had a hammerlock around Joel Kurland's neck. Three of the four were laughing; Joel was mugging for the camera, pretending to be in mortal fear of his life. It was a happy picture, and it created an ache in me that I knew would never quite go away.

I'd never asked Connie to show me a picture of her son, Theo, because I didn't know what kind of reaction that might provoke. But the family had produced five bright, capable offspring, assuring, they thought, a future they could all look forward to with satisfaction. Yet only one of the five was still alive; as Michelle had said, it all came down to Joel. "I wish I'd known," I said ruefully. "I'd have come back sooner."

Connie went over to a large leather sofa and curled up in the corner with a familiarity that told me that was "her" spot in Raymond's study. "You'd have come back? You keep saying that," she said in a voice barely above a whisper. "But you didn't come for Theo's funeral, either. You had to know about it—it was in all the papers. But you didn't even call."

The accusation rocked me. I saw Annette watching me out of the corner of her eye, waiting for an answer. I sat down on the sofa next to Connie and touched her arm. "Connie, I *didn't* know. Not at the time. I was in China when it happened—and even if the story had been in the papers there, I wouldn't have been able to read it. By the time I got back, it was all over and the papers were no longer carrying the story. It was more than a year later before I found out what had happened to Theo."

Connie looked at me with watery eyes. "Oh," she said. "Then you really didn't know, did you?"

I shook my head.

Annette asked, "How did you find out?"

I remembered that well enough. "I was reading a *Newsweek* story about that province in Italy that's made it a felony to pay ransom money, and how that's pretty much put an end to kidnapping there. The article went on to summarize recent cases in other parts of the world where the ransom money had been paid but the kidnap victims were killed anyway. One of them was what they called the Decker case. The story didn't give much in the way of details—just that Raymond had paid the ransom but Theo...Theo didn't make it." Connie twitched but said nothing. I went on, "Then I didn't know what to do. It'd been over a year...I thought if I called, I'd just stir up painful feelings. Open old wounds." In the end, I had done nothing.

Connie was nodding, accepting it.

"What were you doing in China?" Annette asked.

"Directing the tour of a repertory company. The State Department sent us."

Then Annette nodded too, satisfied she had the whole story. "You should have called," she said.

ANNETTE MADE A PRACTICE of checking in with the offices of Decker and Kurland every day, but mostly she was making plans for her trip to Paris. Annette never talked to me about Tom; that was a closed subject. So at first I'd assumed she was going to France to escape the fallout of their separation. But no, it was a business trip.

"What's in Paris?" I asked.

She put aside a prospectus she'd been looking over. "A group of enterprising young men who propose to establish a software distributorship that would cover most of western Europe," she told me in her usual precise way of speaking. "We've been researching the market to see if there's a real need for such a service, and the answer's turned out to be a resounding yes. Now I want to go check out the people themselves."

"Check them out how?" I said idly, only mildly interested. "What do you look for?"

"Obsession," she answered unexpectedly. "If the idea's a good one, and there's a real market need for it, the other ingredient we look for before we invest is obsession. If the people involved in this software distributorship are eaten alive with the desire to make their idea work, then we'll back them. But if it's just another business deal to them—we'll pass."

"Do they know that?"

"Probably. But it's very difficult to fake a real obsession."

"You said a group of enterprising young men. No women?"

"Not in this bunch. Just four young men—in their early to mid-twenties, I'd say."

That made me think of something I'd wondered about before. "Annette, there can't be many women venture capitalists. Does it get in your way, being a woman?"

She'd obviously been asked that before, because she didn't need to think about it. "No, not really. Money's money, whether it comes from a man or a woman. Perhaps I'm remembered a little better than some of the men because I'm a woman, but that's about all." Then she smiled, a big full-blown smile, the first I'd seen from any of the Deckers since I'd come back. "But I'm remembered even more for being a twin. Oh yes—people remember *that*."

I'll bet they did.

ANOTHER TIME, Connie was taking a nap when Annette casually (too casually) asked me if I missed working in the theater.

I said I did, a little, but I had found work that was satisfying. "If someone offered me a plum directing job on a platter, I'd probably take it," I admitted. "But I no longer have the drive you need to pursue jobs in theater. Theater does require a special kind of energy... which I seem to have run out of."

Annette gave me that look out of the corner of her eye again. "Was it worth it?"

The question surprised me. "Of course it was worth it. I wouldn't have missed it for the world."

"Even though you failed?"

It was like a slap in the face. "I didn't fail completely," I told her, hating the defensive note in my voice. "I had some good moments."

She smiled, mouth only. "Good moments. And were those good moments reason enough for turning your back on us?"

Ah, that was it; she resented my not staying with them, just as I'd feared. "I had to try to make a go of it, Annette. Theater is as much my work as your trip to Paris is yours. I've never really left it, you know— my museum is a theater museum. Please understand. I couldn't just sit on my bottom and live off Decker money for the rest of my life."

"But that's exactly what you've been doing, isn't it?" she said in a pleasant tone of voice completely at odds with her words. "I don't recall your turning your back on the money Stuart left you. You never 'suffered for your art'—do they still use that phrase? You had Stuart's money to see you through the lean times."

I couldn't believe she was attacking me like this; I didn't know what to say. "Annette, do you begrudge me the money?"

She made a sound of exasperation. "Of course not! It's your inheritance, you're entitled to it. But don't you see, Gillian? You took from the family what was convenient for you to take, and you took it without offering anything in return...not even your occasional presence. Certainly I can understand your wanting to pursue a career in theater—Stuart was doing the same thing. But that was no reason to cut us out of your life.''

I knew it was only affronted pride that was speaking instead of something more intimate like love betrayed (do they still use that phrase?), but it didn't make any difference. Annette was right, in a way; I did take the money and run. My action must have appeared hypocritical. But I couldn't explain my loyalties were to *one* Decker, Stuart, not to Deckerism as a way of life; telling her that would have been insulting. Oh, lord. What had seemed so clear and clean-cut in Chicago had become disturbingly ambiguous in Boston.

Annette must have read my facial expression correctly because her voice softened when she said, ''That's why you came back, isn't it? To make amends.''

''I came back because I read in the paper that Raymond had died.''

She smiled, this time with her eyes as well as her mouth. ''But you're still here.''

''Yes. I'm still here.''

''And that's as it should be. Here is where you belong, with the rest of your family. No one can live without family, Gillian, and we are yours. For better or worse. And family means responsibilities. Connie called you back because she needs you. We're hoping you'll see her through this trouble.''

What could I say to that? "I'll do what I can," I temporized.

THEN ON THE FIRST DAY of June, I mentioned to my two roommates that I didn't have the right kind of clothing to wear at Martha's Vineyard. Annette jumped at that as an excuse to get Connie out of the house; just the three of us, out for a day of shopping. Girl stuff. I hated shopping; Annette wore only designer originals; and Connie didn't want to go. It was going to be a fun day.

"Where would you like to go?" Annette asked me. "Do you remember any of the stores here?"

"About all I remember is Filene's," I told her. "Stuart and I didn't spend much time in Boston." New York three-fourths of the year, the Vineyard in summer.

Annette was standing in "the twin pose"—hand on hip, one foot forward, head raised. "Well, there's a Nieman-Marcus in Copley Place, and an Yves St. Laurent. Newbury Street has a few places we could go—Louis, or Rae Brewer. Connie, where do you think we should start?"

Forced into making a decision, Connie managed to come up with the name of a shop. Annette chatted about our proposed excursion with an enthusiasm she couldn't possibly be feeling, but Connie eventually began to show some interest. In due course, the three of us set out.

Annette steered us to only those places that delivered so we wouldn't be burdened with packages. Swim suit, short pants, long pants, sporty attire of all sorts.

Several sets of underwear. Reeboks and sandals, thank god. A couple of longish cotton dresses, one of which was so defiantly feminine with all its ruffles and embroidered rosebuds that I could barely keep a straight face when I tried it on; I bought it only because Connie liked it.

Shopping is tiring (that's one reason I don't like it), and only Annette seemed to keep up her energy level as the time passed. Connie's tranquilizer must have worn off because she started talking a blue streak, babbling on about nothing at all. And the more Connie babbled, the slower Annette's own speech became. The difference in the ways those two women spoke told a lot about them. Connie talked in a rush, in half-formed thoughts and sentences that started off on one course and then midway through veered off in a totally different direction—all of which made her sound a bit foolish in contrast to Annette's calm, deliberate, precise speech. Annette was a woman who expected to be listened to; Connie was not.

It was getting on toward two in the afternoon by the time we had everything, and we were all famished. Connie, who was looking quite tired by then, either couldn't or wouldn't express a preference for a restaurant, so Annette chose the Bay Tower Room.

We sat at a table high up in a building overlooking the harbor. I liked being up high; it was restful, sitting above the hubbub, looking down on it and sequestered against its dangers. When the food arrived, Connie began to perk up a little. "Michelle and Rob bought a new sailboat," she said to me. "You'll enjoy that."

"Mm, maybe. Remember, I never learned to sail," I said. "I always just hung on for dear life and let somebody else pull on the ropes."

"They're called lines," Annette laughed. "Sailing isn't all that difficult. Connie could teach you, if you want to learn."

"Yes, I could teach you," Connie agreed. So she was thinking about going to the Vineyard; that was progress.

We'd almost finished eating when a slightly too fashionable man in his forties stopped by our table to express his sympathy for Raymond's death. He told Connie how much he'd miss knowing her husband was there; Raymond had been an important part of a lot of people's lives, and all of them shared her grief. That seemed to be the right thing to say, because Connie actually mustered up a smile for him. The man's name was Patrick Underwood; he didn't look the sort of person who'd have a nickname. Connie introduced me as "Stuart's wife."

I stuck out a hand. "Gillian Clifford," I said without thinking.

We shook hands, enjoying a little friendly eye contact in the process. "Clifford?" he asked, leaving the obvious question unspoken.

"Her professional name," Annette said smoothly. "So, Patrick—what are your plans for the summer?"

I didn't hear his answer; I was too embarrassed by the gaffe I'd just made. Under any other circumstances I'd have maintained that my name was whatever I said it was; but now was no time to insist on an identity separate and apart from the family. *In Illi-*

nois you're a Clifford, I told myself; *in Massachusetts you're a Decker*.

"Perhaps I'll see you there," Patrick Underwood was saying to me.

"Perhaps so," I answered, wondering where *there* was. Martha's Vineyard, I supposed.

During my mental absence Patrick had seated himself at the table with us. Over our postmeal coffee it came out that Patrick owned several radio stations and cable TV companies; possibly he was one of those Uncle Oscar had pressured into leaving the family alone? But Annette had not cold-shouldered him when he first appeared at our table; obviously she didn't consider him part of the enemy camp. A family friend? A lover? No, not a lover; there was neither intimacy nor awkwardness between them. They were just two people who'd known each other a long time.

Then Patrick said something that knocked me for a loop. "Do your detectives have a lead on the killer yet?"

Annette shot a warning look in Connie's direction.

Patrick picked it up. "I suppose the police detectives are doing all they can," he covered. "Waiting is the hard part, isn't it?"

Connie hadn't caught on; she was only half listening, off in some world of her own. Annette saw the expression on my face and made a little hand gesture that I translated as *I'll explain later*. Damn right she would.

Patrick very neatly turned the conversation to me, wanting to know why I had a professional name as well as a "real" one. I told him briefly of my years in

New York theater and of my present position as the curator of a theater museum. ''It was under the name Clifford that I did my directing, and it was that name that got me the curatorship in Chicago. My introducing myself as Gillian Clifford—well, that was just habit, I'm afraid.'' That last was for Annette's benefit. She smiled, barely.

Patrick seemed interested in all this for some reason, and it turned out that he'd actually seen one of the off-Broadway plays I'd directed. He didn't remember much about the play—but that was all right; neither did I. You'd never have known from the polite attention Annette paid to what we were saying that theater bored her to tears. Connie just sat there listlessly, waiting for the conversation to end.

Eventually it did and Patrick Underwood left. Annette immediately signaled for the check and bustled Connie and me out, leaving no time for an awkward silence to develop. Connie did look tired; as soon as we were home I suggested a nap. She agreed. The minute she'd gone upstairs I turned to Annette.

''For heaven's sake, Gillian, don't look at me like that!'' she said sharply.

''You won't tell Connie you've hired private detectives, but you do tell a man who owns radio stations and cable TV?'' I didn't even try to keep the indignation out of my voice.

''It was a defensive move...an ounce of prevention, you might say. Oscar suggested it. He said keep the man at the top informed of what's going on—off the record, of course—and he'll keep the reporters off our backs. So we told Patrick Underwood and a few other people we trust, and they've kept *their* people in line. Everything has been done in strictest confidence. It's how these things are handled, Gillian.''

The way she said my name told me how irritated she was. But I wasn't ready to give it up yet. "Tell Connie. Today. She has a right to know."

Annette shook her head. "Michelle wants to wait until you've taken her to Martha's Vineyard. You'll all be close together there, not spread out the way we are here. Connie's going to need a lot of support." She sighed, half in annoyance and half in regret. "Gillian, you just don't know what she was like the weekend Raymond died. It was as if a raging tiger had been living inside this pussycat for all these years. We handled it the best way we could. She will be told, I promise you."

It looked as if I was going to have to settle for that. And Annette was right about one thing; I didn't know what it was like when Raymond died, I hadn't been there. If I'd had to watch Connie going crazy right in front of my eyes, I surely would have tried to calm her too. Annette was telling me to shut up because I didn't know what I was talking about. All right. But I had another reason for keeping quiet.

So far as I knew, neither of the twins had ever lied to me—until now. But I was as sure as I was that my name was Gillian Clifford that Annette had lied just then; I know acting when I see it. She hadn't told me the truth about why they'd confided what was supposed to be a family secret to a kingpin in the world of mass communication, the last sort of person in the world I'd think they'd trust with a matter they wanted kept quiet. Something else was going on here, something they didn't want me to know about. All the family had appeared so frank and open, welcoming me, sharing their grief, accepting me back into the fold . . . but Annette had lied to me.

Connie Decker wasn't the only one they were keeping in the dark.

SIX

ANNETTE LEFT for Paris. Connie's mood began to lighten. I did not know if those two events were related or not.

But one thing was certain, and that was that Connie was indeed coming out of her funk. Her period of mourning was by no means over; she'd still burst into tears whenever thoughts of Raymond grew too strong. Nights were the hardest for her; she took to sleeping in a bed other than the one she'd shared with him. But that enervating numbness that had surrounded Raymond's death and funeral was dissipating; I could feel it slipping away from me as well.

Before Annette left I tried to get her to tell me about Theo Decker's kidnapping; I didn't have the heart to ask Connie. But Annette made me feel I'd committed some inexcusable faux pas even by asking. That was an ugly and frightening period in all their lives, she said, and they'd coped with it by not dwelling on it. It was over and done with.

Sure it was. Like hell.

For one thing, it would never be over for Connie; even the more recent death of her husband couldn't blot out the earlier heartache of losing a child. And losing a child in that particular way put the whole thing into the realm of nightmare. The pain of Theo's death had been magnified by all the publicity it had received, but that disaster seemed unrelated to what was happening now. On the other hand, I didn't really know that was true. I didn't *know* anything, not even the details of the kidnapping. Annette was right; I should have called.

So when Connie's friend Marcie stopped by for a visit, I told them I had an errand to run; I could at least make an effort to bring myself up to date. Connie didn't think to offer me a car, but that was just as well. From what I remembered of Boston traffic and the rarity of parking spaces, I wasn't any too eager to drive anyway. I called a cab.

My destination was Boylston Street and the Boston Public Library, which turned out to be two separate buildings. My know-everything cabdriver told me the newer building was the circulation library, while the older one housed research materials. I pushed through the revolving door of the old building and came upon the first-floor periodicals section. After a little hunting, I found what I was looking for.

The first account of the kidnapping had appeared in the Boston *Globe* only after the whole tragic story was over; not a word had been leaked to the press while there was still some chance of getting Theo Decker back alive. Theo had been fifteen years old at the time, the same age Joel Kurland was now. A picture in the paper showed a boy who'd even looked like Joel—the face was a little broader, perhaps, the lips fuller, but still a Decker face.

At the time of the kidnapping Theo and his parents had been living in Norway for five months...Norway? The *Globe* said Raymond was there watchdogging an outfit drilling for offshore oil that he'd sunk a lot of Decker money into. (And being Raymond, naturally he'd want his family there with him.) The kidnapping had taken place while Theo was away from home spending the weekend with an American family living in Kristiansand.

Theo and the fourteen-year-old girlfriend he was visiting had been hanging out at the picture-pretty harbor, watching the ships, when a car squealed up to them out of nowhere. Two men had jumped out and wrestled Theo into the back seat, yelling something unintelligible at the girl; a third man had driven the car away. According to the girlfriend, all three were "Mediterranean-looking" and spoke a language she couldn't understand. Immediately everyone thought: *Arabs.*

Whoever they were, they made no move for forty-eight hours, just long enough to push Theo's anxious parents right to the edge of collapse. Then a small box arrived; it contained a school ring Theo wore a lot. The ring was still on Theo's finger. The finger was still attached to Theo's hand.

I had to stop reading for a bit when I came to that. They'd cut off his hand. Just to show they meant business, just to prove they could. A power trip, that's what it was—a sick, dirty power trip. *See, we can do anything to your family we want, and you can't stop us*! What kind of people would do a thing like that? Only animals, the worst kind of predatory animals, with no humanizing restraints to keep them from inflicting harm wherever and whenever they liked. They must have gotten a lot of excitement out of cutting off a fifteen-year-old boy's hand, the three of them.

My mental name-calling didn't make things any better, so I went back to the story. In the box with Theo's hand had been a ransom letter, demanding "an undisclosed amount" of money, the *Globe* said—undisclosed to the public, the writer meant. Raymond paid the ransom, following the instructions in the letter (no details given in the newspaper account). Then Theo was returned to his parents.

One piece at a time.

First a leg arrived, then an arm, and so on. The head was the last body part to be sent. The kidnappers had obviously never intended to let Theo live, but the act of dismembering him spoke of so much hatred at work that my stomach started churning. Was it hatred of Raymond Decker in particular or of ugly Americans in general? Oh, Theo! My god, what he must have gone through *before* they dismembered him!

Follow-ups to the story said the kidnappers were still at large. The only other thing the *Globe* had to add was that Connie Decker had been hospitalized.

No wonder; anybody would go off the deep end after a thing like that—I was surprised that Connie had managed to function at all. And no wonder Annette didn't want to talk to me about it; I'd had no idea Theo's death had been so grisly. Oh Jesus, that poor kid! Poor Connie and Raymond, and poor everybody else too. And I'd been off playacting in China while the family was going through this torture; and because it was death elsewhere, I'd remained untouched by it.

I left the library and started walking, heading east on Boylston past Copley Square. Thank god I'd not asked Connie about the kidnapping, and I would respect the silence Annette had imposed on me for her sister-in-law's sake. Connie didn't have a lot of resources to draw on; I was sure the only way she'd learned to live with what had happened to Theo was to put it all firmly out of her mind. Human kind cannot bear very much reality, the poet said. You got that right, T. S.

I hadn't been walking more than a minute or two before I started getting uncomfortably warm; it was June, after all, and I was working up a sweat. Good. What I really wanted was to hit something, but maybe I could sweat off my tension instead. Right ahead was the Public Garden; I turned in, hoping the stately trees and the flowers in full bloom would lighten my black mood. I passed a young couple trying to persuade their dubious four-year-old that he would reeeeelly love a ride in one of the Swan Boats.

On the face of it, Theo's death would seem to have no relationship to the recent deaths of his father and his three cousins. The newspaper had said nothing about any terrorist organization claiming credit for the kidnapping, although there'd been plenty of speculation about just that at the time. But whatever was going on then, it did seem unconnected to the present tragedies. There were, however, two elements in common between then and now. The first I dismissed as insignificant: all four of the youngsters had been away from home when they met disaster. For all I knew, that was true of all kidnappings; and as for murder—

well, it was bound to be easier to kill someone who was not locked away in the safety of his home. So scratch that; the victim's being away from home wasn't a coincidence so much as it was a requirement, from the criminal point of view. The other element in common was not so easy to dismiss.

Mutilation.

The Deckers didn't follow the barbaric practice of opencasket viewing, thank heaven. But even if they did, opening the casket would not have been possible for any of the four who'd died this year. Bobby and Lynn with their smashed skulls, Ike with his nearly severed body, Raymond burned beyond recognition. Even if the bodies of the first three could have been reconstructed enough to make a presentable appearance, everyone who viewed them would be thinking of the mutilation just the same. Morbidly I wondered what Raymond and Connie had done about Theo's remains. Cremation, I supposed.

Without realizing it I had passed all the way through the Public Garden; I crossed Charles Street to Boston Common, where a lot of student-type people were lolling around, enjoying the warm June weather. I looked for an empty patch and plopped down, heedless of grass stains.

Maybe I just wanted a connection between Theo's gruesome death and what was going on now; that way I'd have an explanation of all the ugliness, a sort of explanation. Mad Arab terrorists, following some logic that made sense only to themselves, out to assure their places in Muhammad's promised paradise of delights by killing rich American infidels in the here and now. How many lives did a ticket to heaven cost?

But it made no sense; Raymond and the three kids had not been killed for glory, for publicity, for satisfying the demands of a power-hungry religion centered on the other side of the world. They were all four *private* killings, done swiftly and mercilessly and without fanfare. No gang of wild-eyed terrorists was running around the northeastern corner of the continent killing Deckers wherever they could find them. No, the reason had to be closer to home.

Perhaps the mutilations that so bothered me were not all that much out of the ordinary, callous as that might sound; perhaps that kind of hate-filled violence was less unusual than I thought. The way of the world now? There was a time in the not-too-distant past when you could go about your business knowing that most of the people you were going to meet in your life would be decent people. But not now. Certainly not now. You'd be a fool to live your life that way now. Barbara Tuchman once said that the Nazi offenses committed against humanity and permitted by the rest of the world had the effect of breaking through some sort of moral barrier—like breaking the sound barrier. It's as though once we understood what evil man was capable of, all the rules broke down.

But if terrorists didn't kill Raymond and the kids, then it had to be one individual known to the family, it seemed to me. So where did that leave us? With copycat killings? Someone who hated the Deckers so much that he chose a way of murdering his victims that was bound to remind them of the way Theo had died? Opening old wounds as well as inflicting new ones? Oh, that was a *lot* of hate. Surely the family would know if they'd made an enemy capable of such outrageous retaliation; how could anyone keep that much hatred hidden all the time? And if the murders were a form of retaliation . . . retaliation for what?

I stood up, brushed off my clothes, and tried to remember where Boston's financial district was. On the other side of the Common, if I recalled correctly. Walking distance; I set out. By the time I reached the Old South Meeting House at the western end of Milk Street, I'd gotten my bearings back.

The buildings on Milk Street weren't especially large, but they imposed their own kind of authority. The firm of Decker Investments, now Decker and Kurland, occupied an old building that had once housed a branch of the long-defunct Second National Bank. The façade boasted the thick columns and heavy lintel that seemed to be the architectural symbol of financial stability everywhere. One of the first things Raymond Decker had done when he'd assumed control of the business was to gut the building. Keeping the exterior intact, he'd had an entirely new structure built inside the old shell—an office designer's high-tech dream of adequate wiring for computers, fax machines, electronic tickers, wrap-around screens, all the other accoutrements of modern business. Going into Decker and Kurland was like entering an ancient Greek temple only to find yourself aboard a spaceship.

Michelle wasn't in, but Rob was. I had to wait ten minutes while he finished a phone conversation; his courteous but unsmiling secretary settled me comfortably with a cup of coffee in a little alcove off the reception area. It was midafternoon; I'd missed lunch, but what I'd learned earlier in the day had pretty much killed my appetite. The brief wait gave me a chance to get oriented. Decker and Kurland was no paper-littered circus of manic rushing and shouting; on the other hand, the pace was not leisurely, either. *Measured* was the word. Efficiency and control were the watchwords here.

Rob came out of his office carrying his own cup of coffee, still looking too thin and ailing. "Ah, Gillian," he said edgily as he sank down into a chair next to mine, "there is a breed of human being that is dedicated to the proposition that contracts were made to be broken. And the breed is proliferating."

"Problems?"

"Oh, a group of whiz kids in Texas is trying to play us off against some other investors they've got lined up. We can't permit that, of course." He took a sip of his coffee. "Now, what can I do for you?"

I told him where I'd been that morning and what I'd learned, hurrying past the details when I saw his face tightening. Rob listened without speaking as I suggested my copycat theory. "It has to be someone who wants to hurt the entire family," I went on, "either some kook insanely envious of the Deckers...or someone you know personally. Has anyone in the family made *that* kind of enemy?"

He didn't answer right away. Then he said in his raspy voice, "We make enemies all the time, every time we pull off a successful deal."

"Anyone crazy enough to kill to get even? Rob, I know you must have gone through all this a thousand times, but remember it's still new to me. I want to know what's been done."

He nodded. "When we first realized the accidents were not accidents, we sat down and drew up a list of all the people we could think of who might bear grudges against us. We turned the list over to our private investigators."

"What did they find out?"

"Not a damned thing, so far. They're still investigating Raymond's death, but they came up with nothing about Bobby's. Or the other two. Too much time had passed, you see. They couldn't trace the whereabouts of most of the people on the list for the times of the murders." A look of pain passed over his bony face. "I'm beginning to think we'll never know who or why."

"Could it be a personal enemy? Instead of a business rival, I mean."

"I wouldn't know who. We're on good terms with most of the people we know—and the others, well, there's no passionate hatred involved. Nothing like this."

"Rob, your detectives had to have found *something*."

He sighed. "You'd think so, wouldn't you?"

"Well?"

He seemed to be thinking it over. Then abruptly he stood up. "Come into my office. I want to show you something."

I put down my coffee cup and followed him. He closed the door behind us and unlocked one of the drawers of his desk, taking out three folders which he handed to me. I opened the top one. ''The detectives' reports?''

''You have the right to know everything we do,'' he said, ''which isn't much, unfortunately. Read the reports, Gillian—read them carefully. Maybe a fresh pair of eyes will see something the rest of us are overlooking.'' He consulted his watch. ''I have a meeting. Stay here, take as much time as you like. We'll talk again later.''

I felt a twinge of guilt as I watched him leave; the last thing Rob needed was for some long-lost relative to show up and start asking questions. But that's what I'd done, and since I'd already asked the questions...I sat down at Rob's desk and opened the folders.

For over an hour I read the reports—names, dates, places, none of which meant anything to me. Everyone the Deckers had been able to think of who might be a secret enemy had been investigated by the firm of detectives they'd hired. Going on the assumption that one person was responsible for all the killings, I couldn't put my finger on any single name on the list and claim that person made a good suspect. One man was known to be in Canada when Ike Henry was killed by a car in Toronto, but he'd been testifying before a Senate committee in Washington when Bobby Kurland was killed on a Vermont ski slope. Another who'd been in New York when Lynn Ferguson was murdered in her hotel bathtub had been recuperating from surgery in a California hospital at the time Raymond Decker burned to death at Martha's Vineyard. And so it went, with all of them; even those whose whereabouts couldn't be verified for one of the killings had what looked like ironclad alibis for one or more of the others.

Of course, there was always the possibility that one of these people had hired someone to do his killing for him. But once you started thinking in terms of contract killings, you were right back where you started— with a list of names. They were names of people who could be guilty as hell or pure as the driven snow, with no way in the world of knowing which. Rob was right; the detectives had, in effect, found nothing.

If this were a television show, I would skim quickly through the reports and pick up immediately on the one seemingly insignificant item that would ultimately lead us to the identity of the killer. But nothing like that happened; I read the reports over and over, and nothing at all suggested itself to me. If anything, I ended up fairly well convinced that everyone on the Deckers' list of potential enemies was innocent. I didn't want to believe that; because if these hideous killings were not motivated by business dealings, that left two equally unpalatable alternatives. One was that the motivation was a personal one and the killer was somebody close to the Decker family circle, a possibility that was even more disturbing than the idea of an impartial avenger out to get his own back because it introduced the element of personal betrayal. The other alternative was that the killer was a crazy whose identity couldn't be reasoned out, or deducted from available evidence, or investigated into existence; he could only be caught in the act.

But that's what we were left with: an unknown nut or a known betrayer. Even the investigating detectives had suggested the person they were looking for would most likely be found among the Deckers' circle of personal acquaintances. One investigator had spelled out his conviction that the killer was no crazy out for kicks; his reason was that the murders had no element of braggadocio to them. The killings were done quietly, under circumstances that could allow the deaths to be mistaken for accidents; but most crazies killed for recognition, the detective said. In that one investigator's mind, there was no doubt whatsoever that the killer was close to or part of the family.

Part of the family?

Well, that was a natural thing for him to think, I supposed. In his line of work he'd probably come across parents who killed their children or worse, if there was anything worse. There was no reason for the investigator to understand the Deckers' obsession with family; most people wouldn't understand it, I imagined. I wasn't even sure I did; but I did know it was real. I knew it was so real that it could stimulate feelings of resentment strong enough to tempt outsiders into taking drastic action of some sort. Look at me; I'd taken action of a more innocent sort when the family got to be too much for me.

Yeah, look at me.

My insistence on a separate life for myself was beginning to look more and more like a child's running away from an overwhelming home life. I'd been a little frog in the big Decker pond, and I couldn't stand that. But I'd never really gotten away. As Annette had rather acidly pointed out, I'd had Stuart's money to see me through what otherwise would have been very lean years in the New York theater. And it was Stuart's money that had bought my house in Chicago.

On a sideboard running along the wall behind Rob's desk was a group of framed photos of Bobby. None of Michelle; that would have been an affectation, I suppose, since she occupied the office suite right next to Rob's. There were six pictures in the group, the first of Bobby as a toddler, then one of him at the age when I knew him—around eight, maybe younger. Then Bobby dressed up as Paul Revere for a school pageant, Bobby on a sailboat, Bobby in what must have been his first tuxedo. The last picture showed the composed and confident face of a youngster who looked older than his eighteen years: Bobby the man.

At the end of the sideboard stood one recent picture of Joel, larger than any of the others. The survivor.

The thought struck me that I wouldn't have known about any of this if I hadn't been reading the obituary notice of a longtime favorite movie star, followed by that startling announcement of *Death elsewhere*. Raymond's obituary had pried me out of my self-woven cocoon and plunged me into a world where people murdered each other. If I hadn't bought a paper that day, I'd still be in my museum, effectively insulated against the kind of anguish the family was suffering and would go on suffering. But now . . . now I was right in the middle of it.

This was not death elsewhere. This was death right here.

SEVEN

DR. TOM HENRY was the first to leave Boston for Martha's Vineyard. Then Elinor Ferguson called and said she and Oscar had just arrived there from Washington. Then the Kurlands went down—Michelle, Rob, and Joel. Only Connie and I were left.

At first Connie seemed relieved to be out from under the family's somewhat smothering concern; she even laughed once or twice. But that didn't last long. In less than a day she began to grow fidgety and started talking about getting away for a while. I suggested Hawaii. Too humid, she said. Montego Bay? Too crowded. Well, then, what about Europe? During tourist season? she asked, aghast. Getting desperate, I suggested she try some place she'd never been before. Valparaiso? Zanzibar? Katmandu? Her eyes moistened and she told me she didn't want to be surrounded by strangers.

Then one morning she announced it was time to go to the Vineyard. The repairs on the house were finished; we could move in any time. I couldn't help but think going there would be a mistake; staying in the house where Raymond had burned to death couldn't be easy for her. But Connie had been too dependent on the Deckers for too long to do without them now; the family's daily phone calls from the island urging her to join them merely helped convince her to do something she already wanted to do in the first place.

We started packing. It turned out to be a bigger chore than it should have been; Connie was having trouble making decisions—what to take, what to leave behind. Once I found her in tears, unable to decide between the brown-lensed sunglasses she held in one hand and a yellow pair in the other. She sat droop-shouldered on an armless upholstered chair in her room, her dark hair falling over her eyes; Connie would be fifty in another three years, but at times she was as helpless as a child. But even someone stronger would have had trouble coping with all Connie had been through, so I told her to go take it easy and I'd do her packing for her. I began to understand why everyone always did things for Connie: it was the only way to get anything done. I packed both pairs of sunglasses.

Connie extracted a promise from me that I would stay with her instead of in Stuart's and my house. I told her we could both stay in my house if she felt uncomfortable going back to the place where Raymond had died. But Connie surprised me; she said she was going to have to face it sooner or later, and it might as well be sooner. I understood, in a way; the Vineyard was a source of mixed feelings for me as well, ones I'd never come close to resolving. If Connie could face up to the ordeal, then so could I.

JUST SMELLING the salty tang of the sea on the crossing was enough to get me excited about being back; the air was bracing and all those other words invented to describe sea air. It felt like years since I'd taken such really deep breaths. I'd been citybound too long; and while I knew I'd start yearning for exhaust fumes and noise and crowded sidewalks before too much more time had passed, the island was what I needed right then. Martha's Vineyard was a retreat from the world, it was security surrounded by water, it was a celebrity hideaway, it was easy living.

Connie and I had brought the Jaguar over on the Woods Hole ferry, which churned into the slip at Vineyard Haven where deckhands waited to open the big metal doors. The streets of Vineyard Haven were full of daytrippers on their rented mopeds and college students there for the summer to work as waitresses, bus boys, and tour guides. Across the harbor I could see West Chop; I headed the Jag in that direction when Connie said she didn't want to drive. The short drive was enjoyable; the island was so seductive, so removed from late twentieth-century hassle and push. Arriving at Martha's Vineyard was like leaving the rest of America behind; the habitués referred to the surrounding water as the moat. The island had no traffic lights, no billboards... and no murders.

No murders, until Raymond. What an appalling way to be remembered, as the only homicide victim on Martha's Vineyard. This would be the first summer the clan had convened here without Raymond... and without Bobby, and Ike, and Lynn. I deliberately put the murders out of my mind. We were here to escape.

Summer was a time for roughing it. The family's idea of roughing it was to leave the help behind in Boston. Oh, someone would clean the houses and stock them with supplies before any of the family arrived, and someone would clean up after everybody had gone home. But in between those two times, the Deckers were strictly on their own—cooking, picking up after themselves, enduring other similar hardships. Spending a few weeks each year without someone to do their grunge work for them was as close to the simple life as any Decker ever got. I used to fantasize about dropping them all into the middle of the Gobi Desert or maybe somewhere in the Australian outback, and then sitting back and watching how they fared. I abandoned the fantasy once I realized they'd probably come out owning the place.

I unlocked the gate in the stone wall that separated the Deckers from the rest of the world and drove us through; no electronic gizmo had ever been installed. Connie was understandably nervous about going into the house where Raymond had met such a gruesome death—and to tell the truth, so was I, a little. We both sat in the car and looked at the place for a couple of minutes. It was a lovely old white frame house, roomy and comfortable, with the original Victorian gingerbread still attached to the bottoms of the various overhangs. It had been the earliest Decker summer home; the other houses had been built as they were needed. Starting with Raymond's grandfather, the head of the Decker clan had always seen to it that the original house was meticulously maintained and even enlarged over the years. There was nothing ominous about the place.

"It's just a house," I finally muttered. "Come on." Connie reluctantly followed me out of the car.

The place appeared isolated, but it wasn't. Just over a small rise to the left was the Kurlands' house, and a grove of cedar trees to the right hid the Fergusons' place. Beyond the Fergusons' was the house Tom Henry had shared with Annette and Ike and where he was now staying alone. And beyond that was Stuart's and my house. All five houses were enclosed within one continuous stone wall. On the other side of the Kurlands there was room for more houses; Joel would be building his own there one day, but the space tacitly reserved for Bobby, Lynn and Ike would go unused this generation.

But the five houses that did stand there occupied a stretch of some of the most desirable waterfront property on the island. Each house had its own pier in back; the kids had used them as markers in swimming contests way back when. It was where young Lynn Ferguson had started developing the athletic skills that ultimately led her to an Olympics elimination meet in New York...and to a hotel room she was never to leave.

Morbid thoughts. I took Connie's key from her and unlocked the door. The house smelled sweet and fresh, as if it had been aired only five minutes earlier. It was only when we went toward the back that we caught the lingering odor of smoke that the new coats of paint hadn't quite been able to soak up. From where I was standing I could see two smoke alarms, one in the hallway ceiling and one inside the kitchen. Raymond had evidently been sleeping in the downstairs guest room for some reason, and it was there the fire had started. Had *been* started. The room was easy to get to from outside. Anyone could have walked along the beach and come up from the back. The killer would have arrived by boat; stone walls couldn't do anything about that.

Connie hesitated in the doorway, unwilling to go into the guest room. "His ankle must have been hurting him," she murmured to herself. "He didn't say a word to me about it."

I asked her what she was talking about.

Connie roused herself, as if only then remembering I was there. "Raymond broke his ankle while we were living in Norway," she explained. "It was about a month before...before Theo." She took a deep breath. "It was a bad break—Raymond was still on crutches when, when Theo was taken. Do you know they don't call them crutches anymore? He was using two of those aluminum cane things, you know what I mean?"

I said I knew.

"Anyway, Raymond's ankle never was right after that. It would hurt him so badly at times, he wouldn't want to climb stairs. He'd always sleep in a downstairs room when that happened."

"Didn't he have any painkillers?"

"He said they made him dopey the next day. He'd take them if it got too bad."

Poor man; physical agony on top of everything else. "What a pity he was down here alone. If one of the others had been on the island to see the flames—"

"Oh, they were all here," Connie said. "It was Annette who called the fire department. I was the only one who hadn't come yet."

That surprised me; I'd assumed all along that Raymond was the only one of the family on the island at the time of his death. I thought back, trying to remember; I couldn't recall anyone's actually *saying* Raymond had been here alone. But no one had mentioned being here when Raymond had died, either. Odd.

There was something that didn't sound quite right about all that, but I couldn't put my finger on it. Connie and I went out onto a rear deck that had been added since I was last there; we both leaned on the railing and stared out at the sea. At the Kurlands' pier to the left, a small sailboat rode easily in the water, its sails furled. There was a breeze blowing in off the water, carrying that wonderful tangy salt odor with it. It was peaceful there, and pleasant; the weather wasn't too hot yet. June was the nicest time of year, I thought.

June...that was what was wrong. It was still May when Raymond had died. "Connie—what was everyone doing down here in May? You *never* come to the Vineyard that early in the year. Or do you now?"

She shook her head. "No, we didn't get here until the end of July last year. Raymond was, I don't know, jittery, all last month. Really on edge. He said he needed a break and came down early."

"But what about the others?"

"That was the strangest thing. They all followed him within a few days. Nobody had said a word about going early, and then—bang! Everybody's in this big hurry to get to the Vineyard. Me, I can't just pack up and go that fast."

"You said everybody was here. You mean Michelle and Annette and their families. Not the Fergusons, surely."

"Oh yes—Aunt Elinor and Uncle Oscar were here too. Some committee Uncle Oscar chairs was still in session, but he left it to come here. He went back to Washington the very next day after Raymond died." Connie's voice was a mixture of indignation and hurt. "But they were all here."

"It sounds to me like some sort of family pow-wow."

"No, it couldn't have been. No one told me. I guess everybody just got the fidgets at the same time and wanted to get away for a few days."

That meant little; Connie was rarely included in the big decision-making. But something had been going on the weekend Raymond died, that was certain. And Connie had been kept out of it, that was equally certain. "Annette and Tom both were here? They hadn't separated yet?"

"They were both here. I think that weekend was when they decided to get a divorce. I'm not sure."

Some weekend. A family conference important enough to pull Oscar Ferguson away from pressing Congressional duties; Annette and Tom's deciding to go their separate ways; the murder of the head of the clan. I was going to have to get someone to tell me what that conference was about. If anyone would.

After a while we went upstairs to unpack and change. My room was at the back of the house, almost directly over the new deck where Connie and I had been standing, so I had an unobstructed view of the sea. The bedroom had a fireplace—a sure sign of the house's age, that plus the wide planks in the floor. I took out the picture of the four kids Connie had given me and put it on the mantel.

When I went downstairs, Connie was making us some tea. She asked me to call everyone and announce our arrival; the numbers were all programmed into the kitchen phone. The Kurlands weren't home; I left a message on their machine. Elinor Ferguson immediately invited us to dinner, an invitation I accepted after consulting Connie. Tom Henry merely said he was glad I'd decided to come.

After we finished our tea, Connie announced she wanted a nap. Connie spent a lot of time sleeping; I had to wonder if she'd slept that often during the day before Raymond died or whether it was just escape from thinking that she was seeking. I wandered down to the narrow beach, wearing wonderfully comfortable sandals—which became less comfortable the minute the sand began to work its way in. I slipped the sandals off; it had been years since I'd walked barefoot on a beach. It was late afternoon and most of the shoreline was in shadow, but the sand was still warm from the baking it had taken earlier in the day.

Raymond had been jittery and on edge last month, Connie had said. Something had been bothering him, and bothering him so much that he had to get away from the others for a while. And yet they'd all trooped down after him. Why? What couldn't wait? And why had Raymond wanted to get away in the first place? Connie obviously didn't know.

I scuffed my way through the thankfully clean sand to the boathouse and peered in through the one small window. It was dark inside; I could barely make out the prow of a boat bobbing gently in the water. Next to it was the white hull of a much larger boat; what kind, I didn't know. Both boats had spent the winter in dry dock, undoubtedly, waiting to be moved here by a crew of the anonymous, highly paid folk who took care of Decker property when the family was away. The boathouse door was locked, so I made my way out to the end of the pier and sat down, my legs dangling over the side. I wasn't in the least tempted to slide into the water; early morning is the best time for swimming.

Then something popped into my head, something Rob Kurland had said. It was the night I'd spent at the Kurland house in Sherborn, when he and Michelle admitted they too thought the accidents were no accidents. Rob said Raymond had been the first to suspect that the kids in the family were being systematically murdered.

Raymond had been the first to suspect. Raymond had been nervous about something shortly before he came to the Vineyard. Raymond had been murdered.

Three facts—were they related? Undoubtedly. Raymond was suspicious and edgy and dead, in that order. Conclusion: Raymond had found out something. He knew, or thought he knew, who was responsible for the deaths of Bobby Kurland, Ike Henry, and Lynn Ferguson. And that's why the killer had interrupted his plan of murdering one youngster a month and had gone after Raymond instead. The killer *knew* Raymond knew.

I felt a tremor of excitement. Raymond had known! But how had the killer found out? Had Raymond let something slip? Not likely; Raymond wasn't a careless man. Perhaps he'd confronted the killer directly... no, that would have been foolish. When you think you have evidence that X is a killer, X is the last person you tell about it.

Whom would you tell? You'd tell the police. Or the detectives you've hired. Or your spouse. Or some other member of the family. Did Raymond really have any material evidence, or had he just put two and two together and come up with the right answer? *And how did the killer know*?

I stood up and began to pace back and forth along the pier. Raymond had been burned to death because he'd figured out who the killer was. And if I could figure *that* out—why hadn't the rest of the family done the same? Or was that just something else they were keeping from me?

Wait a minute—maybe Raymond did tell the rest of the family. Perhaps he hadn't been avoiding them at all when he took off for the Vineyard so early in the year; perhaps he'd called the family conference himself. That would mean that everyone in the family except Connie knew what Raymond had known... but none of them had been murdered. Oh boy, talk about getting nowhere fast. I couldn't make any sense out of this mess. I stopped my pacing and concentrated, going over it again. What had really happened?

After a while the welcome roar of a motorboat cut across my speculations, which were getting more and more convoluted. I looked up to see a tiny craft speedily growing larger as it headed toward the pier where I was standing. As it came nearer I could make out Joel Kurland in the cockpit and Michelle reclining gracefully on the bench behind him like Cleopatra on a motorized barge; they were both smiling and waving. The two were so obviously mother and son, with their dark good looks and identical happy expressions, that I found myself smiling and waving back; I was glad to see them. Joel throttled down and eased the boat alongside the end of the pier.

"Aunt Gillian—hello!" he said at the same time his mother called out, "Gillian! You're here!" Michelle raised both arms in dramatic greeting; she was wearing a white top with voluminous pleated sleeves that made her look like some exotic butterfly poised for flight. They both wore big smiles that told the world they'd been having a good time.

"Hello—I'm here!" I laughed; their good mood was infectious. "We got in a couple of hours ago. Connie's taking a nap."

"Was it difficult for her? Coming to the house."

"Yes, but she's handling it a lot better than I would have expected. I think Connie's going to be all right."

"Terrif!" Joel said with a grin. "Aunt Connie's a lot tougher than you guys give her credit for."

"Oh, is that so," his mother said, tapping him playfully on the shoulder. "Gillian, you don't want to cook your first night here—come over and eat with us."

"Thank you, but we've already told Elinor we'd eat at their house. Where's Rob?"

"He had to go into town to pick up a few things." A breeze lifted Michelle's short hair and dropped it back into place again, perfectly. "What on earth were you so wrapped up in a few minutes ago? You were as still as a statue when we first spotted you."

I stared at the word *Switzer* painted on the hull of their boat and shrugged. "Things."

She caught on. "Well, we'll have plenty of time to talk—about everything under the sun. No hurry. What are your plans for tomorrow? Do you have any?"

"Not yet."

"Take Connie sailing. It'll be good for her."

"I'm afraid Connie would have to take me," I said ruefully. "I can't handle a boat."

Michelle made a small grimace. "That's right, I forgot. You're not as crazy about boats as we are."

Joel made a show of clearing his throat and proceeded to announce somewhat theatrically, "Fear not, Aunt Gillian, for I have just the answer to your problem. I will gladly teach you how to windsurf."

Michelle groaned and laughed.

"How to *wot*?" I said in my best unbelieving Joan Greenwood manner.

"Windsurf—it's cool," Joel went on enthusiastically. "And it's a good way to get started with sailing."

"You mean ride on one of those surfboards with a sail stuck in the middle?"

"Yeah, that's it! It's the closest to walking on water you can get without actually being Jesus Christ."

"Oh, dear—I think I should probably reprimand you for that," Michelle remarked lazily. "Joel, my love, your Aunt Gillian has more sense than to go out on one of those flimsy things. Perhaps something a little more stable would be better."

"They're not flimsy, Mom—and she'll love it."

Somehow I doubted that. "Why don't I just watch you," I suggested brightly.

"Because you're not a watcher." He grinned at me impudently and gunned the motor. "Tomorrow morning, bright and early."

Michelle lifted her hands in a what-can-you-do gesture. They roared off the same way they'd arrived, smiling and waving.

I watched them go, marveling at the change that had taken place in Michelle. The tightly controlled tension so much in evidence in Boston had all but disappeared. She was relaxed, comfortable with her son and her surroundings, and obviously enjoying herself. Getting away from the city's funereal gloom had made one whale of a difference. An amazing difference, in fact: she looked like a woman without a care in the world. What she did not look like was a woman whose only remaining child could still be number one on some unknown killer's hit list. She didn't look like that at all.

The psychology eluded me. Here was a woman who'd lost a son, a nephew, a niece, and most recently a brother—all within the past four months. But perhaps the only way to deal with so much tragedy was to keep it at arm's length. Michelle may have feared she'd lose her self-control if she let herself mourn too deeply. After all, she'd watched Connie go off the deep end right after Theo's death, so seriously disturbed that she had to be hospitalized. But Michelle had the inner resources to draw on that poor Connie lacked; *Michelle* would never end up in a hospital looking to strangers with hypodermic needles for peace of mind. It would never happen to her; she wouldn't allow it to happen.

So I guess it made a kind of sense after all. Michelle's way was healthier than giving in to despair, more sensibly resilient and recuperative. And she was keeping Joel healthy too—that alone was justification.

The beach was now completely in shadow. Time to collect my sandals, go wake Connie, and get ready for dinner with the Fergusons.

EIGHT

OF THE ENTIRE Decker clan, I think Elinor Ferguson loved Martha's Vineyard the most. As a Congressional wife, she was on display every waking minute of her life except for the times she and Oscar managed to slip away to the island. Aunt Elinor honestly enjoyed the display aspect of her life; she'd chosen it, after all, thereby revealing that Decker streak of theatricality that was so much more noticeable in Michelle and Annette. But even people like Elinor who thrived on public life needed a hideyhole on occasion. As for Uncle Oscar, he'd once said the Vineyard was the only place in the world he could take off his shoes and put his feet up without being stared at as if he'd just grown a second head.

I didn't see how they did it. Knowing you were constantly being judged—not only on what you said but how you said it, on the way you looked and the way you handled a dinner fork, on where you put in an appearance and where you didn't...it would drive me nuts. They were never allowed to have bad days, or feel tired, or even look as if they did. All that on top of their real work: Oscar's helping make the country's laws and Elinor's running the Decker Philanthropic Foundation. Within the family, Elinor's was considered the more important job.

Elinor met us at the door, announcing that Oscar was in the kitchen. She gave Connie a warm hug and me a polite peck on the cheek. She looked good—relaxed and strong and elegant all at the same time, even in her casual summer clothes. She'd be around sixty now, or close to it; Oscar was a couple of years younger, I remembered. "Oscar still likes to cook?" I asked, mostly to help the conversation along.

She gave me a conspiratorial wink. "Yes, and I don't want either of you doing a thing to discourage him! He doesn't often have the time to indulge and it does give me an excuse to stay out of the kitchen. So brag on everything. Please!"

"That won't be difficult, from what I remember of Oscar's cooking."

We'd reached the kitchen. "Did you hear that, dear?" Elinor asked her husband. "Gillian remembers your cooking."

Oscar was standing at the stove with a ladle in his hand, handsome and imposing even in this setting; he managed a bow in my direction without dripping any sauce on the stove. "I always knew Gillian was a woman of taste and discernment. Connie—come say hello."

Connie went over for a second hug. "What are we having, Uncle Oscar?"

"Lobster. Plucked live from the trap just this morning."

Connie made an *ugh* face. "I don't want to hear about that part of it."

What would we do without food—not to eat, but to talk about. Oscar used his rich actor's voice to hold forth on one of his favorite subjects. Lobster, clams, the right sauces, the wines to go with them, the proper amount of time to marinate fava beans, when to serve white asparagus and when green—all that kept the talk carefully neutral until we were seated at the table and tasting Oscar's latest culinary wonder. He really was a good cook.

When Oscar had finished a short disquisition on the proper way to select melons, Elinor turned the conversation to me. "Don't you miss working in the theater?"

One of the twins had asked me the same thing. "Yes and no. Mostly no. Except on the days when it's yes."

She laughed. "Do you think you'll go back to it?"

"No, I'm pretty sure I won't. I have a museum to run now. That's where I belong."

Oscar smilingly threw me an oh-yeah? look. "What about all that *once it's in your blood* et cetera?"

"Well, it is a *theater* museum I'm running. I'm still in the business, in a way."

"You never did any acting, did you, Gillian?" Elinor asked.

"A little, when I was first starting out. It wasn't very satisfying, I found. Actors have so little control over what the audience sees on the stage—they don't even control their own roles, not completely. I'd rather run the show than be in it."

Elinor nodded, understanding.

"I'd be scared to go out on a stage," Connie offered. "In front of all those people? Whoo."

"Well, I'm glad you have work now that you find satisfying," Elinor said to me. "But I have to admit

I've never understood the mystique surrounding theater myself."

Probably because there was so much theater already in her life. Oscar announced he'd done something marvelous with apricots for dessert, and we were back to food again.

When dinner was finished, Elinor hustled Connie off somewhere—to do a little mothering, I suspected—and Oscar suggested we take our after-dinner drinks out on the deck (he called them postprandial libations.) From the deck I could look left and see the lights we'd left on in Connie's house, but the Kurland place on the other side was behind a little spit of land that hid it from view. I looked in the other direction and saw one light in the next house. "How's Tom doing?" I asked.

Oscar took a swallow of his drink before he answered. "He's going through a bad patch right now. Keeps to himself a lot. Sits in that house or takes long walks alone. Ellie's been trying to bring him out of himself a little, but I tell her it's something he's got to work through alone."

"Connie says he and Annette decided on a divorce the same weekend Raymond died."

He frowned. "I don't think so. Seems to me they'd already made up their minds before that."

"Before you all came to the Vineyard for that big family conference? When Raymond died?"

The only light on the deck came from inside the house, but I could make out Oscar looking at me quizzically. "You know about that conference?"

"Only that there was one. Raymond got here first and all the rest of you followed him. You even left work unfinished in Washington to come."

"Connie told you all that?"

I nodded. "What was the conference about, Oscar?"

He swallowed the rest of his drink. "Some unsettled family business."

"Such as who had been killing the kids in the family?"

I could feel his shock there in the semi-darkness. "Where did you get an idea like that?" he finally said.

"Raymond found out something, didn't he?" I persisted. "He thought he knew who the killer was. That's why he called the conference. And that's why *he* was killed, because he knew."

Oscar let out a low moan. "Gillian, Gillian—I'm afraid you've been jumping to conclusions. In the first place, Raymond didn't call that conference. I did."

"*You* did?"

"I did." He paused, getting his thoughts in order. "Look, I don't want you to repeat any of this until I say so. Will you give me your word?"

"Of course."

"I'm getting ready to run for the Senate." He waited while I caught my breath—*Senator* Ferguson! I wasn't really surprised, though; it was a logical progression. I offered my congratulations.

Oscar accepted them as his due and went on, "Obviously I need a larger voting base than just my Congressional district, so for the past few years we've all been working toward lining up additional support. I called the conference because that week I'd just won the endorsement of a labor bloc that could put me over the top. It seemed like the right time to declare my candidacy—that's what the conference was about."

I could understand why the Deckers wanted a Senator in the family; they'd probably started planning for this eighteen or twenty years ago, when Elinor and Oscar were first married. "What did you decide?"

"We didn't. Raymond was killed before we could reach a decision, and everything else had to take a back seat to that. Then I had to return to Washington immediately, to finish up some business before Congress adjourned."

"I don't mean to be nosy, Oscar, but since you were going to adjourn so soon—why not just wait until then to call a family conference? Why *that* weekend?"

"Ah, that was the whole point. I wanted to be able to go back and announce my candidacy privately to certain key people in Washington while we were all still there together. It wasn't essential to do it that way, but it would have made a good dramatic move. Alas, it was not to be."

I got up from where I was sitting and moved over to lean against the deck railing. It was beginning to get chilly; I wished I'd brought a sweater. "Okay, I was wrong about the family conference. But I could be right about why Raymond was killed, couldn't I? Connie said he'd been nervous and jumpy right before he died. That sounds to me as if he'd come across something incriminating and then was killed for it. Surely you must have wondered about that?"

Oscar joined me at the railing. "We considered it, but no one could really believe it. If Raymond had found out something, he would have told us. Immediately. Why would he keep a thing like that to himself?"

I could think of one reason, but it sickened me so much I couldn't bring myself to say it. Instead, I told him I'd read the private investigators' reports Rob Kurland had shown me and asked if they'd come up with anything about Raymond's death since then.

The answer was no. "They're floundering, just like the rest of us. Nobody saw anything or heard anything. We're a little off the beaten path out here, you know. The only people the detectives could question are members of the family—we have no other near neighbors here."

"So it's a washout."

"Looks like it."

We were both silent for a moment or two, and then I mentioned the photograph of the four youngsters Connie had given me. "Lynn was a lovely girl, Oscar. What a terrible waste."

"Waste isn't the word for it. There *isn't* a word for it." His face was in shadow, but I could imagine his expression. "Did you know she campaigned for me the last time I was up for re-election? She was only sixteen then, but that slip of a girl would stand up and face those huge audiences—and they weren't always friendly ones, let me tell you—but face them she did. And most of the time made them listen to her. She had a lot of courage, my daughter did."

I wished I could have seen that—coltish young Lynn facing down a crowd of skeptical voters. "Did she like campaigning?"

"She loved it, Gillian—absolutely loved it. I've never seen anyone take to politics as quickly as Lynn did. She was a natural."

I interpreted that to mean Lynn was being groomed to take her father's place as the family's link with Washington. But now that plan was scotched, just like the plan to make Bobby Kurland a venture capitalist and Ike Henry a research scientist.

"Ellie was over forty when Lynn was born," Oscar murmured, more to himself than to me. "No more children, for any of us. It's all for Joel now." He looked at me sadly. "It's too bad you and Stuart didn't have kids."

"That's what I told her once," Elinor said from the sliding doors that led to the deck. "Remember that, Gillian? You got a little annoyed with me, as I recall."

"Did I? I don't remember." She came over and joined us at the railing. "Where's Connie?"

"Connie's in one of the bedrooms having a good cry. I just told her we'd hired private investigators to look into the deaths in the family."

At last! "And it upset her."

"Well, it's a relief too, you know. It means the family agrees with her and that something's being done. At the same time it's stirred up a lot of anxieties that I think were better left alone."

"That sounds as if you didn't want her to know about the detectives."

Elinor sighed. "No, she has a right to know. And when the girls asked me to tell her, I couldn't very well refuse." The "girls"—forty-five-year-old Annette and Michelle. "She'll be down in a few minutes. She just needs a little time to compose herself."

"Er, do I know about the detectives?" I asked.

"I'm supposed to be telling you now," Elinor said with a smile in her voice. "I'm sorry you've been forced to dissemble like this, Gillian, but there's no longer any need for pretense. And you seem to have gotten stuck with babysitting Connie—we do apologize for that."

"Oh, I don't mind. Connie just needs a semi-outsider to talk to once in a while."

There was a pause, and then Oscar asked, "Are you? Still a semi-outsider? Or are you back for good?"

I was startled; the idea had never occurred to me. As gently as I could, I told them I was staying only until Connie was back on her feet, and then I'd be returning to Chicago.

CONNIE WAS IN A STATE of exhilaration by the time we got home. "They believe me, Gillian! For once they all believe me!" Her eyes were glistening and she moved in quick, nervous gestures.

I didn't like it; she was starting to behave the same way as when I first arrived. "Don't count on too much. They haven't turned up anything, you know."

I might as well not have spoken. "They never listen to me . . . but this time, this time I'm right! They think Raymond was murdered! I knew it! I knew it!"

"Connie, settle down—there's something I want to ask you about." With an effort she calmed herself. "You told me Raymond came down here that weekend because he was edgy and keyed up and just wanted to get away from the city for a while."

"That's right. What about it?"

"That wasn't the reason, Connie. He came down for a family conference. Oscar called it. That's why they were all down here so early in the year."

She stared at me blankly. "It couldn't be. No one told me there was a conference."

Oh Connie, Connie! "Probably because it was a spur-of-the-moment thing," I said in a lame attempt at being tactful. "Do you remember what Raymond told you? His exact words?"

She frowned, prettily. "He said he was going to come down with a bad case of the heebie-jeebies if he didn't get out of Boston for a few days. I remember that. He didn't say a word about any family conference."

"You're sure?"

"Positive."

"Well, maybe Oscar decided to call the conference after Raymond was already here," I said. "That would account for it." We were in my bedroom and I was tired; it had been a long day. The bed looked inviting, but Connie wasn't ready to go yet.

"It still doesn't explain why I wasn't informed," she pouted. "They don't ask my opinion at these meetings, but they never shut me out. All they had to do was pick up a phone."

"You were going down the next day anyway, weren't you? Didn't you tell me you had some errands to run in Boston?"

"Actually, they were Aunt Elinor's errands. She asked me to pick up a couple of proposals from groups that were petitioning the foundation for grants of one sort or another. Aunt Elinor said she wanted to look them over during the weekend. What was the conference about, do you know?"

"Oscar thinks it's time to declare his candidacy for the Senate."

Her face lit up in pure pleasure. "Oh, I'm so glad! It's time, is it? Good, good. I always felt so bad about that other time."

"What other time?"

She threw me a quizzical look. "That's right—you wouldn't know about that. Oscar was all set to go once before, but then . . . well, that's when Theo was killed. Raymond told me later that the family decided not to go ahead."

Later. When she was out of the hospital. "Did he tell you why?"

"He said because there were sure to be people who'd accuse Oscar of capitalizing on a family tragedy. To get the sympathy vote." Then something happened to her face; she looked as if she were in pain.

"What is it? Connie?"

She swallowed and said, "I just remembered something else he said. Raymond said he thought the rest of the family was naive to assume there'd *be* a sympathy vote to quarrel over. He said the more common reaction would be one of, oh, some German word—he meant people would get pleasure out of our misfortune."

"*Schadenfreude*?"

"Sounds like it. Isn't that terrible? Just because we're Deckers?"

"Yes, that is terrible."

"He must have been wrong. People aren't that meanspirited, are they?"

"No, of course not." I thought Raymond was probably right, but there was no need to say so; Connie'd just start getting agitated again. At the same time I was a bit amused with myself, with how easily I'd fallen into the usual family pattern of *soothing Connie*. She'd been cast—or had cast herself—in the role of the perennial child that must always be protected.

Eventually she went to her own room and I was able to get to bed. But as so often happens when you're dead tired, your mind just won't shut up and let your body get the sleep it needs. I was still learning things about "my" family, such as Theo's untimely and grisly death thwarting Oscar's first attempt at running for the Senate. But what was nagging at me the most was Connie's being shut out of the family conference.

I'd been to several of those conferences back when Stuart was still alive, and Connie had never been excluded from them; the family was just too courteous for that. She never contributed anything, but she was always *there*. But it certainly did look as if they hadn't wanted her on the Vineyard for that last conference. So had Oscar lied to me about calling the conference himself, ostensibly to determine the next step in his political career? Raymond had lied about why he was going, and Elinor had invented an excuse to keep Connie in Boston one more day. They didn't want her there.

Raymond had figured out who was doing the killing and—if Oscar was telling the truth about that— had kept the knowledge to himself. But if Raymond had found out who was behind it, why hadn't he said so? The only answer could be that he'd been protecting someone, trying to work out a solution that would put an end to the killings without exposing the killer. He wouldn't do that for a business rival. As much as it sickened me to think it, that meant the killer had to be a member of the family.

Only one member of the family had been deliberately excluded from that last conference. Perhaps Raymond had asked Elinor to find something that would keep Connie in Boston while the rest of them were meeting on Martha's Vineyard. Why? The answer seemed obvious. Because Connie was the one he was protecting.

Connie?

The idea was so stupid I laughed out loud. Connie Poor-Little-Me Decker, actually undertaking something as complex and daring as a series of murders! One thing I do know something about is acting, and I knew Connie was not *acting* the role of a passive, doless woman. She could no more undertake the committing of murder than she could swim from Boston to Miami. She wouldn't kill, not because of her moral standards (which I presumed were as high as anybody else's), but simply because she'd never be able to handle the detail work. All those things to think of, and plan out ahead of time, and keep straight once they were planned, and then actually *do*? Not our Connie; not in a million years.

Sleep was impossible. I got out of bed and pulled on a pair of trousers over the tail of my nightshirt, thinking that I simply must stop making these idiotic assumptions and suppositions. Look where they'd led me: to big bad Connie Decker, murdering other people's children because she went off her rocker when her own child was killed. Sick, Gillian, sick. Suddenly I felt an urgent longing for a place where I once was happy, where family members didn't start thinking other family members might be homicidal maniacs. I wanted to see Stuart's and my house.

The moon lit the road running just inside the Decker-protecting stone wall fairly well, but I could have done with a flashlight just the same. I passed the grove of fragrant cedar trees, Elinor and Oscar's house, and Tom Henry's house, where one light was still burning. Then it was there, my house, silhouetted by the moon-bright ocean behind it.

It was the smallest and most modern of the five Decker homes; Stuart had built it only the year before we met. We used to keep a spare key in a tin box hidden around back, but I wouldn't be needing it. All these years I'd held on to my own key; I'd given copies to the twins when I left. Only now did it occur to me that the family might have had the lock changed. But no; the key wouldn't go in at first, but then it did and it turned easily. The door clicked open.

I stood there in the dark a few moments, trying to calm the fluttering in my stomach. Creeping back in the dead of night was not the way I'd envisioned returning to this house; but there I was, so I might as well get on with it. *It's only a house*, as I'd earlier said to Connie about her own place. I felt for the switch and turned on the light.

And saw Tom Henry pointing a gun at me.

"*Tom!*" I screamed.

His face turned white and he lowered the gun quickly. "Oh my god, Gillian! I'm sorry! I thought someone was breaking in!"

"No! I have a key!" I held the key up stupidly, as if justifying my right to be there. I was upset, to say the least.

Tom put the gun down on a table and came over to grasp my shoulders. "I really did give you a scare, didn't I? I am so sorry!"

"Of course you gave me a scare! No one's ever pointed a loaded gun at me before." I took a deep breath and willed myself to calm down. "It is loaded, I assume?"

"Unfortunately, yes. You must forgive me, Gillian. It's just that . . . I've been a bit jumpy lately."

Well, of course he had—and more than a bit, if the gun was any evidence. "It's all right, Tom. No harm done. What are you doing here?"

His hands dropped away from my shoulders. "I've been having trouble sleeping. The last few nights . . . well, I do better if I can just get away from *there* for a couple of hours." He jerked his head toward his own house. "A different bed under a different roof helps. I apologize for intruding, Gillian."

He must have used the key we'd kept hidden out back; either that or the twins had had copies made for everyone. "You're not intruding. No one's using the place—you might as well sleep here. But I saw a light on in your house."

He gave me a wry smile. "That's for the Fergusons' benefit. I leave it on most of the time. Elinor tends to fuss if she doesn't know where I am."

I was thinking. "Why don't you just move in, if you're more comfortable here? There's no reason you shouldn't."

"Thanks, but that won't be necessary. It just gets bad at night. But as long as you're here—how about some coffee? Or cocoa? Or maybe a drink."

"No, no—this was a bad idea. The middle of the night isn't the best time for a nostalgia trip. I was having trouble sleeping too. I'll come back tomorrow."

"Don't go—"

"Yes, I must. Good night, Tom." I fled.

I practically ran all the way back to Connie's house, barely able to see the road under my feet. Poor Tom. He'd obviously wanted company, someone to talk to... and my running out on him was not only ungenerous, it was unkind. But I'd had all I could take for one day; enough was enough. Besides, I didn't want to turn into that one family member that the others feel they can always go to with their troubles.

And that too was ungenerous.

It wasn't until I was back in bed that I realized I'd actually been in Stuart's and my house for the first time in ten years . . . and I hadn't seen it. The furnishings, the fittings, the little odds and ends—I hadn't seen a thing.

All I'd seen was a man with a gun.

NINE

I WAS AWAKENED the next morning by a brisk ratatat-tat on my bedroom door. Assuming it was Connie, I called out to come in; but no, it was Joel, overflowing with the kind of youthful ebullience that's always slightly obscene that early in the day.

"Time to get up, Aunt Gillian!" he announced with unbearable morning cheeriness. "You don't want to be late for your first windsurfing lesson, do you?"

First? Of how many? I peered at him through one eye. "What time is it?"

"It's daytime. Time to be moving!"

I looked out the window and saw a blanket of gray. "Is that fog?"

"It'll burn off by the time you have your other eye open. Come on, Aunt Gillian, put on your swim suit. Let's go!"

"Joel," I said firmly, "I'm not going anywhere or doing anything until I've had some coffee."

"Already thought of that," he said smugly. "I started a pot before I came up to get you. I'll wait in the kitchen." Then before I could protest, he was gone.

I'd managed to forget how the family always made themselves at home in each other's houses on the Vineyard. Joel wouldn't have dreamed of letting himself into his Aunt Connie's Boston house without permission, but here he probably even had a key. Being awakened by a fifteen-year-old boy eager to go do something wet, chilly, and undoubtedly hazardous was not my idea of a great way to start the day. But I pulled myself out of bed and went through my morning ritual. When I'd put on my new swim suit and cover-up, I stopped by Connie's door. No sound; still sleeping. I followed the aroma of fresh coffee down to the kitchen.

Joel was eating blueberry muffins and drinking milk; I poured a cup of coffee and sat down at the table with him. "Admittedly I am no expert on New England weather and related phenomena," I said, "but that still looks like fog out there to me."

Joel swallowed a mouthful of muffin and said, "It's already lifting. It's not much of a fog anyway." He placed one spread-fingered hand on his chest and proclaimed dramatically, "'The fog comes on little cat feet.'"

"Um. I bet Carl Sandburg never had a cat walk on him while he was trying to sleep. Joel, is this windsurfing stuff absolutely necessary?"

"Absolutely. You said you wanted to learn to sail, didn't you?" I hadn't exactly said that. "Well, this is an easy first step," he went on. "You learn to control one sail before you move on to something more complicated. Besides, it's fun. Prepare yourself for the thrill of a lifetime!"

"Thrills I don't need. Another hour's sleep would be nice."

"Too late. You're going windsurfing and you're going to love it."

And my mother's a duck. But I finished my coffee and the two of us left by the back way for my lesson in windsurfing. Joel was right about the fog; it was lifting fast. I followed him along the beach between Connie's house and his own until he stopped before a couple of boards with furled sails. I started to make some ironic remark about how he just happened to have two boards when I realized one of them must have been Bobby's.

Michelle had called them flimsy, but up close they looked pretty solid. Still... "Joel, I don't know about this—"

"Don't say no till you've given it a try, Aunt Gillian. And don't worry, nothing's going to happen. This is a good place to learn—the winds are gentle here. If you want big waves, you have to go upisland. Besides, the wind's blowing toward the land right now, so if you mess up you'll drift back toward the beach instead of out to sea."

"Oh, that's a comforting thought."

"That one's yours," he said, pointing.

White board, red-and-white sail. "It's a lot bigger than the other one."

"It's an entry-level board—bigger means more stable. Bobby and I both learned on that board."

"Wait a minute—yours has footholds and mine doesn't!"

"I took the footstraps off that board. You'll be moving around a lot until you get the feel of it. Most beginner boards don't have straps at all. Look at that! The sun's out. Now we can get started."

Hurray, hurray.

We pushed my board out until we were standing waist-deep in the water. The mast puzzled me; I'd always expected well-behaved masts to stand upright in one spot and not move about, but this one was built to pivot all over the place. Joel lowered the centerboard—which he called a daggerboard—and unfurled the sail, which promptly drooped down into the water. "Is it supposed to do that?" I asked.

He assured me it was. "We'll start you off by uphauling. Hop aboard."

Hop? I pulled myself up on the board and put one foot on each side of the mast. The board that had looked so big on the beach now seemed *awfully* small. Following Joel's directions I "climbed" the uphaul line, hand over hand, until the sail and mast were completely out of the water; they looked heavy as all get-out but were surprisingly light. Then Joel had me lean back slowly to allow the water to drain off the red-and-white sail. It felt as if I were going to topple over backwards at any moment, but it didn't happen.

Then my lesson started in earnest. The boom was a curved rail to hold on to while sailing, but Joel had me start out by grabbing the mast with both hands right under the boom. I learned to tack; I took tiny little steps around the mast while swinging the sail toward the back of the board. The result was a 180-degree turn...it worked! Then I reversed the procedure, swinging the sail around toward the front to jibe back in the direction I was originally facing. Joel made me practice those two turns until I was ready to scream at him; I was itching to get going.

At last Joel had me pull in the mast until it was right over the center of the board; only then was I allowed to grab the boom. Joel shouted, "Go! And remember to keep your knees bent and your back straight!"

I went. Oh, I went like the wind! The rig tended to pull me into a stiff-legged posture so at first I had to concentrate on keeping the proper stance. But then I got the hang of it and didn't have to keep thinking about it. And it was splendid, simply splendid! I know simple planing like what I was doing was kid stuff in the eyes of the experts in the sport; but to someone out on a board for the first time, it was glorious! How could anything be so exhilarating and so relaxing at the same time? It wasn't long until I was looking around for rougher water.

Joel appeared on his board, his yellow-and-green sail billowing out in front of him. "How do you like it?" he called.

"I love it!" I yelled back. "You were right!"

"Ready for a little race?"

I was. At least I thought I was, but we'd barely lined up before something started to go wrong. I could feel the sail pulling me over and let out a howl.

"Let go with your back hand!" Joel shouted.

I did, but it was too late. Over I went into the ocean with all that board and rigging over my head. The sun hadn't had time to warm up the water yet and it was *cold*. I swam to a clear spot in the surface and came up to find Joel laughing like crazy.

"Look on it as a baptism, Aunt Gillian!" he called. "Has to happen to everybody. Now start over."

He wouldn't lift a finger to help me, but kept circling and talking to me while I went through the whole rigamarole by myself. I got the board right side up, climbed on, uphauled, drained the sail, positioned the mast, grabbed the boom, glared at Joel, and announced the race was on. The two of us planed along side by side, until we passed the point of land we'd agreed on as the finish line. The race was a tie. Whoever said fifteen-year-old boys couldn't be diplomatic?

I didn't quit until the muscles in my legs began to cramp. I waved to Joel and headed in. Once on the beach, I let the sail down; then I let myself down, very gingerly, and started massaging my calves. Joel was still tacking and jibing effortlessly, farther out from shore now. Another sail appeared, this one attached to a real boat; I could see a teenager on board, waving and calling something to Joel. The two youngsters rode the water in small circles, staying close enough to talk. After a few minutes the sailboat slid gracefully away.

What if that had been a man with a gun?

Alarms went off. I'd been suppressing thoughts of danger for too long; now they all but swamped me. It was so easy to be lulled into a false sense of security, especially when you want to be lulled. But nothing had changed; there was still somebody out there who was killing Deckers.

I looked out at Joel, balanced on top of the water with nothing but a glorified surfboard between him and drowning. Exposed, vulnerable, an easy target for someone with malice in his heart and a rifle in his hands. Anyone could come along and put a bullet in Joel, and that would be the end of the Massachusetts branch of the Decker line. Was that what this was all about? Somebody wanted to kill off the entire family? Destroy the younger generation and the whole family dies.

If I were Joel's mother, I wouldn't have let that boy out of my sight for one minute. And yet both his parents let him go about his business as if nothing were happening, as if none of them had a care in the world. Why weren't they more on guard? Why weren't they all banded together in some impregnable fortress, armed to the teeth and determined to defend themselves at all costs?

"Are you having fun?" a voice said from over my head.

I twisted around and looked up at Tom Henry standing behind me. "Hello, Tom."

"You looked like a kid out there, Gillian. I was watching from the back deck." He hunkered down beside me. "What's wrong with your leg? Cramp?"

"Muscles I don't use much are acting up, I guess."

"Here, let me." His gentle surgeon's fingers probed the calf of my leg until they found the knotted spot and then gently worked it loose. "How's that?"

"Much better—thank you." I felt I owed him an apology. "I'm sorry I ran out on you last night." I stopped him when he started to protest. "My only excuse is that it had been a long day, and when I saw the gun . . . well, I got rattled, that's all."

He shook his head. "I'm the one who should do the apologizing. I use your house without permission and then I wave a gun at you. Can you forgive me?"

"Oh, you *had* permission, Tom—to use the house, not to wave the gun. I told the twins when I left that it was the family's house from then on. But about that gun...do you actually carry it with you when you can't sleep at your own place?"

He gave a sad little smile. "No, I keep one there, and one in my own house as well. Paranoid, huh?"

Sensible was what I'd call it, and I said so. "You're taking precautions, which is more than the others are doing. Not like the Kurlands—they act as if there's no danger at all."

"It's their way of coping. Keep pain at a safe distance and it can't destroy you. The twins have always been like that, never letting things get too close. And Rob..." He trailed off with a shrug.

"Rob's another twin."

Tom actually laughed at that. "It seems that way sometimes, doesn't it? Rob might as well have been born a Decker—he's certainly become one."

We fell silent, watching Joel skimming along over the surface of the water. He disappeared around a little spit of land; and when he came back two other windsurfers were with him, two boys of about his own age, I thought—it was hard to be sure at that distance. They were trying to work out some maneuver in unison, but the wind died on them.

"They are special, aren't they?" Tom murmured.

He didn't mean the three boys, or at least not all of them; he was talking about the Decker clan. *They*, he'd said. Tom must have been feeling more and more like an outsider the closer he came to his divorce.

I looked at the man sitting next to me. Tom had always been a little different from the rest of the family. He didn't have the flair for the theatrical that the others had, for one thing. Maybe because he didn't need it; it seemed to me Tom had more solid accomplishments under his belt than any of the rest of them. This man saved lives, not money.

But even Tom's appearance was different. He was of average height instead of tall like the others. He'd probably have a weight problem when he got a little older; the Deckers never would. That curly, sandy-colored hair stood out like a lighted match in a dark room among all the ebony-haired Deckers. The Deckers tended to marry people who fit their own physical type; Rob Kurland was the perfect example. Connie was tall and dark-haired; Oscar Ferguson had been too until his hair turned gray. And yes, I fit the pattern as well. I was taller than most women; and while my hair wasn't that shiny Decker black, it was a dark enough brown to satisfy the requirement. I'd once teasingly accused Stuart of wanting to marry me because I had the right look. He'd never really denied it.

And here sat Tom Henry, probably feeling every bit as much out of it as I did. Attracted to the Deckers, but wanting to break free. Preparing himself to leave, but hanging on just a little longer. I wondered if anyone ever really walked away from the Deckers.

We heard a *Hello*! and turned to see Michelle coming down the steps to the beach. She was wearing white shorts and a simple white top that probably cost more than I earned in a month at the museum. Tom sighed, quietly; he had to see Annette every time he looked at her sister.

Michelle came over to us in a casual lope that she managed as easily on sand as she did on solid surfaces. "Gillian, I'm truly sorry Joel put you through that. Windsurfing, of all things! I should simply have forbidden him to bother you."

"I'm glad you didn't." I grinned up at her. "I liked it." And I liked the look of astonishment on her face.

"Well, you're still full of surprises, aren't you?" Her tone of voice made it a friendly remark. "Tom, I haven't seen you in two days."

He waved a hand. "Just didn't feel like coming out of the house."

"Well, you're out now—and about time, I say. Gillian, I want you to bring Connie to lunch. Twelve-thirty, thereabouts. Rob's in Vineyard Haven right now, but he'll be back by then. You haven't made other plans, have you?"

"I haven't. And I don't think Connie has, either."

"Good. Let's keep her as busy as we can until she finds her own pace again. And Tom, I expect you to lunch too."

"Oh, no, Michelle. I don't think so."

"Now, don't say no. I want you to come—we all do. Gillian, tell him to come."

Oh my. "I'd like for you to come, Tom," I said obediently.

Tom looked straight into my eyes for a couple of moments without saying anything. Then he turned to his other sister-in-law and said, "All right, Michelle—I'll be there."

The obviousness of that little interchange made me uncomfortable. He wouldn't go for Michelle, but he would go for me. I wasn't at all sure what that meant.

WHEN I'D DRIED OFF, Tom went back to the house with me to say hello to Connie, only to find she had a guest. The visitor was a woman in her seventies—small, wiry, with short iron-gray hair and skin like a roadmap. She was a longtime friend of the Decker family, but for the life of me I couldn't recall her name. She was wearing a denim skirt and white sneakers, and it came to me that that was what she always wore, even ten years ago when I knew her. Only the shirt varied.

Connie fluttered her fingers at Tom and said to me, "You remember Mrs. Vernon, don't you, Gillian?"

Vernon, that was it. "Of course I do. How are you, Mrs. Vernon?" Her first name was Florence or Thelma or something old-fashioned like that, but no one on the Vineyard ever called her anything but Mrs. Vernon. In this playground of unceremonious living, she was always and ever *Mrs*. Vernon.

The redoubtable Mrs. Vernon came over and planted herself in front of me, barely reaching my shoulder. "So you've come back, have you?" she said. "Well, I hope you have sense enough to stay this time."

Dear Mrs. Vernon. Tom stepped in quickly and said something cordial to the old lady, letting me escape having to answer. Mrs. Vernon had a bluntness to her speech that the rest of the family claimed to find amusing and/or eccentric; I simply found it irritating.

But blunt she was, and she went right on being blunt. "I was just telling Connie that she ought to bypass the usual mourning period. Raymond wouldn't want her to withdraw into a cocoon—would he, Tom?"

"Probably not," he conceded.

"So don't stay shut up in this house all the time you're here," back to Connie, "but stir yourself, go out every day, try to live a normal life. *Do* things, Connie dear."

Connie dear smiled at her; she seemed to like being told what to do in this no-nonsense way. "You're most likely right."

"Damn right I'm right. You mustn't let yourself brood. You feel a depression coming on—nip it in the bud! Exercise, do something physical!"

"We had talked about going sailing," Connie answered vaguely. "Gillian wants to learn how."

Mrs. Vernon looked at me in surprise for not knowing how to sail, but then shook her head. "No, not sailing. That's not sweaty enough. You need something more physical, like tennis. You and Gillian play a couple of sets every day and you'll stay out of the doldrums, you'll see."

"I don't play tennis," I said without thinking.

The older woman stared at me. "You don't sail, you don't play tennis—what do you do?"

I stared right back. "I think beautiful thoughts."

Again Tom stepped in, and this time I wished he hadn't. "You should have seen her windsurfing about an hour ago," he said with a laugh. "She was able to keep up with Joel—and that takes some doing!"

Don't justify me, Tom! But Connie looked at me with curiosity and said, "I'd forgotten that's what you were doing. How did it go?"

"I liked it," I admitted sheepishly. "It's a kid's game, but I did enjoy it once I got the hang of it."

The stern look faded from Mrs. Vernon's face. Windsurfing might not be up there with sailing and tennis, but at least I was making an effort. "Well, I'll be going," she said. "I want to talk to Oscar and Elinor. Are they home, do you know?"

"Oscar's sunning himself on the beach," Tom said. "I don't know where Elinor is."

"Either one will do." Tell one, tell all; Mrs. Vernon knew all about the lively communication network the family maintained. "We've got a fight on our hands this summer. McDonald's is going to make another try."

Tom groaned, and Connie said, "But I thought all that had been settled several years ago!"

"So did we, dear. They must have found some new legal ammunition or they wouldn't be back."

I wasn't sure I understood. "McDonalds—people or fast food?"

"Fast food," Mrs. Vernon said indignantly. "We fought 'em off once before, and we can do it again! But it's going to be harder this time."

Tom walked her to the door and I wished her luck; fast food franchises were so out of keeping with the character of the Vineyard that I was surprised McDonald's had the nerve even to try. No, on second thought, I wasn't surprised.

"Were you really able to keep up with Joel?" Connie asked me.

I shook my head. "He let me. Being nice to the neophyte."

"We'll have to help," Tom said, coming back from seeing Mrs. Vernon out. "More particularly, Connie, *you'll* have to help. Everybody in West Chop knows you and likes you. You're just the one to rally the troops."

A look of something like panic crossed Connie's face. "Oh, I don't think I should . . . it's so soon after the funeral and . . ."

"Connie, listen to me. Mrs. Vernon was right, you know. You need to get out of yourself. It'll be good for the family and you'll be helping the Vineyard as well."

She mewed like a kitten. "I don't know, Tom . . ."

"I'll make you a deal," he said with a smile. "I'll stop moping in my house if you don't start moping in yours. You help Mrs. Vernon, and I'll help you. What do you say?"

"Sounds like a good deal to me," I volunteered. "I'd go for it, Connie."

She looked back and forth between the two of us and then smiled anemically. "Well, all right."

"Good!" Tom said with forced heartiness. "We'll get together with Oscar and Mrs. Vernon and map out a strategy. Unless she's already got one planned, which wouldn't surprise me in the least. Either way, we've got our work cut out for us."

"All right," Connie repeated, but this time more in the spirit of things. "Where do we start?"

"Next door," I said. "Lunch with the Kurlands."

TEN

ROB KURLAND was looking a hundred percent better than the last time I saw him. He had the beginnings of a tan and some color in his cheeks, and his bones no longer seemed ready to poke out through the skin. Even the rasp had gone from his voice. He was healing.

Joel wasn't there (eating at a friend's house, his father said). Talk around the lunch table centered mostly on the upcoming fight against the exploiters and despoilers, as Michelle put it. Once I caught Rob and Michelle exchanging a glance over Tom's animation and Connie's interested compliance. Everybody was healing.

During a lull in the talk, I asked, "Were those the same sneakers and denim skirt Mrs. Vernon was wearing the last time I was here?"

Michelle laughed. "There's a rumor that she gets them wholesale from L. L. Bean. I've never seen her wear anything else—have you, Rob?"

He said he hadn't. "She could buy L. L. Bean out of her pocket change. I guess she just wears what's comfortable."

I said, "I forget—does she live here all year round?"

"She does now," Tom answered me. "She used to be just a summer resident, like us. But then—oh, six or seven years ago—she moved here permanently. When she wants a vacation, she goes to Boston. All of seventy miles away.''

A summer resident *like us*, Tom had said. He still thought of himself as part of the family. Michelle evidently noticed it too, for she picked that moment to say, ''I got a call from Annette this morning. We were expecting her back this week, but she's been delayed.''

Tom looked up from his plate. ''Anything wrong?''

''Not really. She ran into a little snag with three of the four bright young men she was investigating in Paris.''

''The software distributorship,'' I said, remembering.

''Oh, she told you about it? Well, it seems only one of the four has all the ideas. The other three are just leeching on to a good thing. Annette's trying to persuade the idea man to dump the other three.''

''That reminds me,'' Rob said, patting his mouth with a napkin. ''I'm going to have to spend the afternoon on the phone. The Mirren-Whipps deal,'' he said to Michelle. She nodded.

''Working on your vacation?'' I asked.

''There are no vacations in ventures,'' Connie remarked in a mechanical tone of voice. It must have been something she'd heard Raymond say.

Rob smiled. ''Something ventured, something gained. What are your plans for the afternoon, Gillian?''

''I thought I'd go look at our house.''

Connie looked uneasy. "I didn't give you much chance to say, but would you rather stay there? I mean, if you want to—"

"No, Connie. I just want to look at it."

They all understood. No one offered to accompany me, bless them.

FINALLY SEEING the house Stuart and I had shared for two summers was something of an anticlimax. The place looked smaller than I remembered; I thought that was supposed to happen only when you went back to a house where you'd lived as a child. I wandered through the rooms, looking for some personal memento of the time I'd been staying there. There was none. I did find some clothing in a few of the closets, both men's and women's, of various sizes—kept there for guests, no doubt. It didn't feel like "my" house. It was just an extra, temporarily unoccupied building in the Decker compound.

I wondered how many people had stayed here in the ten years I'd been gone. Some of the furniture I didn't recognize, and the window furnishings were all new. The family wasn't letting the place run down; who knew, it could be used again someday, on a permanent basis. Someday. It was a good place to live— warm and comfortable and conveniently appointed, in beautiful surroundings. Maybe Mrs. Vernon had the right idea, living on the island all year round. I gave myself a little shake; no, I wasn't going to fall into that trap again.

The phone rang, making me jump. It was Elinor.

"I'm sorry to disturb you, Gillian," she said, "but something completely slipped my mind. My assistant is flying in from Washington—in fact, her plane should be arriving just about now. We'd meant to put her up in your house, but now that you're back we don't like to do that without your permission."

"Of course she can stay here, Elinor. I'll be staying with Connie as long as I'm here." And Tom would have to find another place to go on nights when he couldn't sleep.

"Oh, that's very gracious of you! Thank you, Gillian. Why don't you come over and meet her? She'll be here about a week, unless problems come up that we haven't anticipated."

I told her I would. When I'd hung up, I sat thinking for a few minutes. My lunch companions hadn't wasted any time telling Elinor where I'd be that afternoon; it was starting to feel as if they were keeping track of me. No, that was paranoid; they told one another everything. The Fergusons had plenty of room to accommodate a guest or two or six, but they'd probably grown used to putting all their visitors in my house. More convenient, not having an outsider underfoot all the time; nicer for the guest, too, having more room. It could all be explained away.

Elinor's mention of her assistant reminded me I hadn't spoken to *my* assistant for a while, so I called Leonard at the museum in Chicago. He said he was very glad to hear from me (the liar), because a sketch of the stage setting for the first production of *Ghosts* had just been found in somebody's attic and was up for auction. I forgot all about the Deckers when I heard that. Ibsen's *Ghosts* had been turned down by the playwright's own theater in Oslo, and by theaters in Sweden and Denmark as well; that stark drama was just too daring for its day. So the world premiere of this landmark play took place at Aurora Turner Hall in Chicago, of all places, in a Norwegian-language production for an audience of Scandinavian immigrants.

And now after all these years a piece of the scene design had turned up—only one page, Leonard warned me, and it looked like a preliminary sketch at that. I questioned him closely about authentication procedures and ended up as convinced as I could be that the sketch was the real McCoy. Leonard and I talked budget and decided how high he should bid; I gave him my Martha's Vineyard phone number and wished him luck.

What a find! I was dying to tell someone about the sketch . . . but whom? None of the family knew anything about theater history, or cared. It was probably just as well. I didn't know if Leonard could outbid the competition; and it wouldn't do to get all excited about something that could very well end up in somebody else's museum.

Frankly, I was worried. Leonard was competent enough to oversee the day-to-day operation of the museum; but the more I thought about it, the more reluctant I grew to leave the bidding at the auction to him. All the big boys would be after the sketch; that long-ago production of Ibsen's gloomy drama wasn't just Chicago theater history, it was world theater history. If Leonard let this one slip through our fingers...

I couldn't let that happen.

MRS. VERNON WAS BACK the next morning; she swept Connie up and away to launch the island-wide campaign to stop the infidel McDonald's from corrupting the Vineyard's chosen way of life. About midmorning I wandered through the cedar grove to the Fergusons', next door. It was a lazy sort of day, the kind that makes you want to watch other people work.

Elinor and her assistant were hard at it. The assistant's name was Nancy Younger; she was in her early twenties and was one of those women I think of as professional porcelain dolls. Delicate features, small bones, translucent skin—everything about her looked breakable. From Elinor's introduction I gathered I was supposed to know Nancy's family; I smiled and uttered something vague.

"About ready to take a break?" I asked Elinor.

"Pretty soon—we have something we have to decide first. Why don't you sit in? We'd welcome your opinion." Uh-huh. At least she didn't say *input*. I sat down at the table with them.

Nancy handed me several sheets of paper. "These are requests for funds from two competing educational groups," she told me in a whispery voice. "We have to decide which one to fund."

"Why not both?" I asked. The Decker Philanthropic Foundation could afford it.

"They both want to use the same physical facility," Elinor sighed. "A Boston high school with well-equipped shops. Both these groups have the admirable goal of teaching carpentry, wiring, and the like to adults who have no job skills. But the school is willing to allow the use of its equipment only one night a week, so we have to say which group goes in—since they both need money for supplies." Small potatoes.

"We've tried to get the two groups to combine," Nancy whispered, "but there seems to be some sort of rivalry between them."

"That's the polite way of putting it," Elinor said dryly.

I looked at the papers Nancy had given me; they were photocopies of application forms that had been filled in by hand, and they were barely literate. One group called itself the Organization for the Advancement of Street People, while the other was Jobs, Ink. I couldn't see much difference between them, but I didn't know the background. I asked about them.

It seemed the OASP was better organized and had been around longer, while Jobs, Ink. was noisier and more visible. The latter had been on television a lot, Nancy said softly, and had attracted a lot of attention to themselves with their angry denunciations of an established social order that failed to take care of the less fortunate among them. I knew right then which one would get the Decker money they both wanted, but I suppose Elinor felt she had to go through the motions of making an impartial decision. The noisy group would win, and in return they'd understand they were expected to mention the Decker Philanthropic Foundation every time they were on TV in the future. That was the one kind of publicity the family wanted.

I only half listened as the two women talked, watching Nancy's hands as she leafed through the papers on the table. They were slender hands, with long delicate fingers with pronounced pads on the tips. I could just see Nancy as a child, wearing a pretty dress and sitting at the piano obediently practicing her scales to the tick of a metronome as her mother stood by watching approvingly. Nancy was probably a good little girl who always did what she was told.

When Elinor asked me what I thought, I put in a plug for the OASP just to be perverse. Not that it made any difference; Elinor took a calculated, roundabout way of talking herself into awarding the grant to Jobs, Ink., but she ended up right where I thought she would. "Well, that's done. I think we can take a break now. Did you want to see me about something, Gillian?"

"Yes," I said, shooting a covert glance at Nancy.

Elinor nodded and said, "Let's go check on Oscar. Nancy, perhaps you'd get us some lemonade?"

We went out on the deck and looked down to where Oscar was sunning himself on the beach and talking on a phone. "I wanted to ask about Connie," I told Elinor. "That time she was hospitalized—right after Theo was killed."

"Oh, yes, that was a dreadful period. Poor Connie. She just couldn't cope. She was hospitalized for only two weeks, I think it was, just long enough for the doctors to draw up a proper diet for her and make sure the medication they prescribed had no side effects."

"Then she didn't undergo therapy?"

"No. Why do you ask?"

Instead of answering her question, I asked another of my own. "Do you think she's really recovered?"

"Gillian, no one ever really recovers from a thing like that. But Connie has accepted what happened to Theo, the same way she's now accepting Raymond's death. Why? Have you seen something in her behavior...?"

"No, nothing like that. She's just...Connie. How did she behave toward Lynn after Theo died?"

"Lynn? The same way she always did." Puzzled.

"She displayed no hostility toward her, or avoided her? Connie showed no resentment that your child was still alive while hers was taken from her? By violence?"

"Why, no, of course not—" Elinor broke off as she understood what I was getting at; her face fell slack with astonishment. "Oscar told me you suspected Raymond knew who the killer was...and was protecting her? Connie?"

I looked at the dismay in her face and said, "Stupid, huh?"

"More than stupid, Gillian—it's shocking! Connie is the most inoffensive person on the face of the earth! Besides, can you possibly imagine her taking all the steps necessary to kill Lynn and the others? Can you?"

"No, I can't," I admitted readily. "I know it's a dumb idea, and I don't for one minute believe that Connie ever hurt anybody. But Raymond had to be protecting *someone*. Otherwise he'd have told the rest of you what he'd found out."

"You're guessing." I just looked at her. Elinor took a deep breath and said, "That's all any of us can do, I suppose. We'll probably never know the truth."

"And you concede to that?" Now it was my turn to be dismayed. "Why aren't you turning the world upside down trying to find this killer?"

"What would you have us do?" she said sharply. "We've cooperated with the police. We've hired private detectives. The one thing we haven't done is start accusing one another." I flinched. But she wasn't finished yet. "You have no idea what we've been through, Gillian. You come in here at the eleventh hour and you say why haven't you done this and why haven't you done that—you think we haven't considered *every* possibility? Do you think we haven't been over and over it time and again?" With an effort she stopped herself. "You must realize what a strain this has been for all of us. I know you're concerned—I'm sorry for my outburst."

"Oh, Elinor, don't apologize! I know I'm butting in, and—"

"You're not butting in! You have every right to be concerned." She tucked a lock of hair behind one ear, taking her time. "You are part of the family, after all. In fact, that reminds me. Oscar wants a family conference. We have to make a decision about announcing his candidacy."

Ah. "When?"

"Tomorrow. We'll let you know the time."

I hesitated. "I may be leaving tomorrow." I told her about the *Ghosts* sketch and my reluctance to leave the bidding to my assistant.

"Can't you bid by phone?"

"I could, but I've never seen this sketch, you know. I'll need to inspect it before I can commit myself to shoot the works."

"But you'll be back?"

I didn't answer immediately. Then I said, "Connie doesn't need me anymore. She's coming out of her slough of despond, and Mrs. Vernon is going to be keeping her pretty busy with this McDonald's thing. I think she'll be all right."

Elinor raised an eyebrow. "You're not worrying about staying under the same roof with a possible murderer, are you?"

"Of course not," I said, embarrassed. "I was fishing. I know Connie's no killer."

Elinor sighed. "Well, if you're determined to be off tomorrow, we'd better hold the conference tonight. That'll give us a chance to try to persuade you to come back! Let's make it nine o'clock—is that all right with you?"

I told her that would be fine.

"There's Nancy with the lemonade." We went back inside and each of us took a glass of the ice-cold drink Nancy had just poured. "Mm, that's delicious," Elinor said. "Now, if you two will excuse me for a moment? I'll be right back."

I sat down at the table across from Nancy and looked at those long thin fingers again. "Do you play the piano?"

"Why...yes, I do," she whispered. "How did you know?"

"You have a pianist's hands." She looked pleased. I didn't mention that the best pianists I'd ever heard had short, stubby fingers that curled into claws when they played. "How long have you been working for Elinor?"

Almost five years, she said—which meant she was older than the twenty-one or -two she looked. We made polite, bland conversation until Elinor came back and resumed her seat at the table. She picked up one of the subliterate proposals we'd been muddling over and said, "Just look at this! Whatever has happened to the teaching of the English language? Not one sentence written correctly!" She shook her head in dismay. "The spelling is abominable, the grammar is atrocious, and the punctuation—oh my. They have no *idea* what punctuation is for!"

That was the moment Joel chose to come charging in through the deck doors proclaiming that he was dying of starvation and what did we plan on doing about it? He was wearing shorts and a tee shirt that said *To hell with the prime directive; let's kill something.*

Elinor nodded approval at the semicolon and told him to help himself. When Joel had disappeared in the direction of the kitchen, she laughed and said, "Why is it all fifteen-year-olds are such whirlwinds? Well, back to business. Nancy, we'll need the standard recommendation form for the board. Then a polite-regrets letter for the Organization for the Advancement of Street People."

Notifying the foundation's board of directors was only a formality; the members had been chosen for their willingness to rubberstamp Elinor's decisions. She and Nancy moved on to the next petitioner, and I started looking for a tactful way to escape.

Joel came back in chewing on a sandwich and announced, "Tom's here."

Tom Henry followed his nephew in and raised his eyebrows when he saw me. "Gillian! You're helping distribute alms to the worthy?"

"Just sitting in for a moment," I said, standing up.

"Hello, Tom," Nancy said in a tiny voice.

"Tom, I'm glad you're here," Elinor said. "Gillian wants to go back to Chicago tomorrow—you must talk her out of it."

Both Tom and Joel said *Oh no* and started listing reasons why I shouldn't go. I half listened to them and half watched Nancy. She was gazing at Tom with a tentative smile on her lips and a glow in her eyes that gave away much too much of what she was feeling. Tom spoke to her courteously but distantly. He had to know, it was so obvious.

"So you see, you *can't* go," Joel announced firmly, and brought me back from speculating about Nancy.

I moved toward the deck doors. "Elinor and Nancy have work to do."

"Right," said Tom. "Come on, Joel, we'll work on her outside."

"Goodbye, Tom," Nancy said faintly.

It wasn't until we were on the steps down to the beach that it hit me. Elinor excuses herself from the

room and five minutes later Tom Henry shows up.
Just like that.

   She'd called him. She'd called him, to come over to
the house...and do what?

ELEVEN

JOEL GOT IT into his head that another hour or two of windsurfing would make me change my mind about going back to Chicago. Tom went with him to set up the boards; I wanted a word with Oscar first.

Uncle Congressman Oscar Ferguson was basking in the sun on the beach and still talking on a phone—using his politician's voice, I noticed. I sat down on the sand next to him and waited until he'd finished charming whomever he was talking to. He wound up his call and pushed the antenna down. "Well, Gillian. Glorious day, isn't it?"

"It is indeed. A good day to declare your candidacy." I grinned at him. "Congratulations."

"Why, thank you. But that won't be until tomorrow."

"If you're thinking about the family conference, that's going to be tonight. My fault, I'm afraid. I may be going back to Chicago tomorrow."

He shot me a look. "Oh, I hope not. You just got here."

"Business."

"Can't be taken care of by phone?"

I shrugged. "How do you plan to announce your candidacy? Press conference? In a speech you're scheduled to give somewhere?"

Oscar smiled. "The word is 'address'—politicians don't make speeches, we deliver addresses. As to when and where, that's one of the things we'll have to decide tonight."

"Then it's settled you're going ahead with it?"

"Pretty much. About time, too."

I drew a picture of a sailboat in the sand. "I was wondering about that. I'd have thought you'd have made your move long before this."

Oscar shifted his weight in his beach chair before answering. "I was on the verge of declaring my candidacy once before—about four years ago. We'd talked it over and were all ready to go." He stopped talking and pressed his lips together.

"What happened?" I knew Connie's version; I didn't know if it was right.

He made a rumbling noise, not quite a sigh. "Theo happened. The kidnapping and the murder...they pushed everything else aside. Declaring then was unthinkable."

Atrocious timing; of course he couldn't announce he was running for the Senate while all that was going on. "But later?"

"Even a year later people were still talking about it. We were afraid if I announced then, I'd be regarded as exploiting my nephew's death to gain public sympathy. And a year after that, a lot of my support had slipped away. There's no such thing as a lifetime commitment in politics. So I had to start rebuilding."

Theo, Theo—even now his death was affecting this family. "Oscar, I want you to tell me the truth. Do you think the people who killed Theo are the ones who're responsible for what's been happening this year?''

"No."

"You said that awfully fast."

"No."

"But what makes you so sure?"

He lifted his sunglasses and stared at me. "I *know* they're not responsible. Because they're dead, Gillian. All three of them."

That astounded me so, I had to ask Oscar to repeat part of what he said next. It seemed that the three men who killed Theo were nothing more than sadistic, second-rate criminals. They were Lebanese—at least two of them were; there was some question about the third. But they'd been trained somewhat in the ways of terrorism, and had in fact been expelled from one of the more "respectable" terrorist groups—good god!—for unreliability and lack of discipline.

"How do you know all this?" I asked.

"CIA investigation."

"CIA? How'd they get involved?"

"I called them," Oscar said simply.

So after being expelled, the three pseudo-terrorists had decided to strike out on their own. They made up a name for themselves, the People's Alliance for Justice, and proceeded to work an extortion racket on whatever Europeans they could convince that the PAJ was a large organization for which they three were only the contact men. Their victims were small merchants, mostly, people without the resources or the connections to fight back. The three political terrorists manqués proceeded to kill and dismember two men who'd resisted, as an object lesson, ostensibly; the CIA thought it more likely they simply enjoyed their work. One of the two who'd been killed was the owner of a small fleet of fishing boats, a Norwegian.

That's what had brought the three Lebanese (one questionable) to Norway, where the presence of the rich American infidel Raymond Decker gave them the idea of trying their hand at kidnapping. The CIA had no hard evidence that these three had killed Theo, at least no evidence the authorities in Norway would recognize; but there was no question in the American agents' minds that those particular men were responsible, and those three alone. Maybe the three of them thought they'd be welcomed back by the terrorist organization that had expelled them if they could demonstrate, once again, the helplessness of the American government in the face of foreign harassment; the CIA had turned up some slight evidence to that effect.

Or, maybe they just wanted the money.

Whichever it was, the CIA reported to Oscar that the three didn't get to enjoy the ransom money they'd extorted from Raymond. The car they were driving south through France went over a cliff; all three men were killed instantly, a convenient and timely solution to an otherwise insoluble problem. Oscar said the CIA had not exactly been forthcoming with the details.

I shivered in the sunshine; it was a cold story Oscar had told me. ''The *Globe* said Theo's killers were never caught.''

"Well, they weren't. Three Levantines die in a driving accident in France. Taken at face value, there's nothing to connect that with Theo's murder."

I shivered again. "Do you think the CIA...?"

Oscar slowly levered himself out of his beach chair and stretched his arms over his head. "I don't know, Gillian. And I don't think we want to know. But those three men never even got their names in the European papers. To the faithful, that's even worse than going to meet Muhammad wrapped in a pigskin."

I stood up and brushed the sand off my backside. "How much was the ransom?"

"Some outrageous sum. Twenty million, I think."

"Twenty million!"

"They had something to prove, you see. Maybe they thought they could buy their way back into that group, the United Armies of the Prophet or whatever the hell they called themselves. It might have worked, too."

"What happened to the money?"

"The CIA recovered most of it. The rest...who knows? Gillian, it's over and done with now. Don't dwell on it, and for god's sake don't start talking about it to Connie."

"Don't worry, I won't."

"I have to go in before I start looking like a lobster. Are you all right?"

I was sick to my stomach, angry, dizzy, and frustrated. "I'm fine."

"Look, there's Joel—I think he wants you to go windsurfing."

THE WINDSURFING was a bust. I couldn't concentrate on what I was doing, my head was so full of images of the CIA tracking down those three men who'd killed Theo and . . . doing what? Raymond's millions hadn't been able to save his son. The money didn't matter when put in balance against a life; but it seemed pretty clear that no powerful, well-organized terrorist group was behind the three kidnappers/killers and was now out for revenge against surviving Deckers.

The board and sail I was struggling to control seemed slippier and less manageable than the other time I'd tried Joel's favorite water game. What had been so exhilarating my first time out was now just plain rocky and precarious and a little bit scary. When I got dumped into the water for the third time, I gave up. I dragged myself and the board up onto the beach where Tom stood watching.

He wasn't alone. Elinor must have released Nancy Younger from her chores, for there she stood talking animatedly to Tom in her little-girl voice. Tom looked *very* glad to see me and ran to help with my board. Any other time I would have found that funny.

"What happened?" he wanted to know as I wrung the water out of my hair.

"Oh, just couldn't get going. Joel's going to give me an *F* for today."

"I thought you did very well," Nancy whispered generously. "Joel's coming in too."

I watched my nephew making his graceful approach to the beach, thinking again of how vulnerable he was out there on the water. He hopped off his board, lowered the sail, and shook his head at me sadly. "Not good, Aunt Gillian. You weren't concentrating."

"I know. I had something on my mind."

"But you don't feel beaten, do you? *Do you*?" He repeated it so insistently that I hastened to assure him no indeed I was not discouraged. "You have to expect a setback or two," he said. "You're making a good go, Aunt Gillian, honest. Now Tom here—he's too chicken even to try."

"Am not," Tom said in mock indignation. "It's just that I prefer sitting down when I'm handling a sail."

"Uh-huh," said Joel.

Nancy spoke up, as much as Nancy ever spoke up. "I was telling Tom about a restaurant in Vineyard Haven that's under new management. It's really a first-rate place to eat now. Really."

Tom took a deep breath and said, "Yes, it sounds good. What do you say, Gillian? Want to give it a try? We'll have time for a bite before the conference tonight."

I saw the look of disappointment on Nancy's face and thought Tom could have found a more subtle way of rejecting her. "I don't know, Tom. Connie—"

"Is eating at our place tonight," Joel interposed. "I heard Mom talking to her on the phone. You go ahead with Tom—I'll tell 'em where you are."

"That's settled, then," Tom said with ill-concealed relief. "Come on—I'll wait for you while you get dried off and change. Ah, Nancy? Excuse us, please? See you tomorrow, probably." He grabbed my elbow and steered me in the direction of Connie's house at an unnecessarily hasty pace. Joel trotted along with us.

I waited until we were out of the range of Nancy's hearing and said, "That was unkind, Tom."

He groaned while Joel laughed. "You don't know the background, Aunt Gillian," the latter said. "Nancy's had the hots for Tom for the last year—"

"Joel," Tom said in a tone of reprimand.

"Well, she has! She sighs and goes all dewy-eyed every time he walks into a room." Tom rolled his eyes. "It's been like that for a long time. Everybody thinks it's a riot."

I wondered how funny Annette had found it.

"Nancy just doesn't take hints," Tom explained. "She's a nice girl, but she lives in a restricted world. I don't think she sees many people other than Deckers."

"Fate worse than death," Joel agreed cheerfully.

Maybe so, but still... "I don't like being used, Tom."

Tom groaned again. "Not my day, is it? I wasn't using you, Gillian. I was going to suggest we go out for a bite anyway. Nancy's talk about the restaurant just provided an opening."

I shrugged and changed the subject. "Joel, your folks told me you had a bodyguard for a while. What happened to him?"

"Them. Three of them, worked eight-hour shifts. It was just impossible, Aunt Gillian. They stuck to me like glue, even followed me to the john at school! Everybody was avoiding me... you'd think I had the plague or something. It was lousy, really lousy, all the time they were there. Mom and Dad finally let them go.''

"When were they let go?''

"When? I dunno, I don't remember.''

"Before Raymond was killed or after?''

"I said I don't remember.'' Impatient tone. "Tom, do you remember?''

Tom shook his head.

"Why do you always call him Tom?'' I asked Joel peevishly. "You call me Aunt Gillian and everybody else Aunt and Uncle, but you never say Uncle...oh.''

They both laughed at me. "That's why,'' Tom said with a smile as we came to Connie's house. "Now you go up and change—I'll wait downstairs.''

AS IT TURNED OUT, we skipped Nancy's restaurant in Vineyard Haven; that otherwise lovely town is dry as a bone. We ended up at the yacht club in Edgartown, where the food and wine were good and the service exemplary. I was glad Tom had suggested it, even though his motives were still a mite questionable; it was nice getting away from the Decker compound for a couple of hours.

Halfway through the meal I said, "Tom, there's something I want to ask you. The night Raymond died—it was Annette who called the fire department? Is that right?''

"Yes, that's right. Why?''

"Well, why Annette? I can understand why the Kurlands didn't turn in the alarm, because of that little hill between their place and Connie and Raymond's—they might not have seen. But the Fergusons are right next door. There's nothing separating them except that grove of cedar trees."

Tom frowned. "Oscar and Elinor were out that evening, if I remember correctly. Annette was too, and she saw the fire as she was coming home. I was in bed asleep and didn't know a thing about it until Annette came running in screaming that Raymond's house was on fire." He paused. "By the time we got there, it was too late."

"She called the fire department before she went to see if Raymond was in the house?"

"Yes," Tom said with a puzzled look. "Wouldn't you?"

"No. I'd go look for Raymond first."

He gave me a sad little smile. "Would you really? If you saw a blazing house, the first thing you'd do is go running into the flames looking for someone to rescue and think about calling the fire department later?"

"Put that way, maybe not." I was silent a minute. "I'm sorry to spoil your dinner by bringing this up," I said to Tom. "I know this is ground you must have covered a thousand times, but I'm still trying to figure out what happened. How could someone set fire to the house without waking Raymond up? I saw two smoke alarms near the room where he died. And he was sleeping downstairs—he should have been able to get out safely."

Tom shook his head. "Not if he'd taken a pain pill. He'd broken his ankle several years ago and it still bothered him at times. The medication tended to make him groggy."

"Yes, Connie told me about that. Did he take a pill that night?"

"I don't know."

"Wasn't there an autopsy?"

Tom reached across the table and took my hand. "Gillian, there wasn't enough of him left to examine." I flinched; he squeezed my hand. "I know, it's painful. But I saw what was left of the body myself. There was no possibility of a postmortem examination."

"So there's no way of knowing?"

"No."

I withdrew my hand. "Didn't the fire start right in the room where Raymond was sleeping? Why would someone risk getting caught like that?"

"Ah, Gillian, that might have been part of the 'thrill' of killing. Someone who sees his mission in life as ridding the world of Deckers ... someone that unstable might view the danger as some sort of personal test."

"Like landing a boat in the dark and sneaking up to the house without being seen?"

"Well, yes, I suppose so."

"Do you really think that's what happened?"

"What else could it have been?"

"It could have been someone in the family."

We stopped talking when the waitress appeared to take away our plates and bring us coffee. Then Tom said, "Is that why you were asking about who called the fire department? Because you suspect Elinor and Oscar? Or Annette?"

"Oh, Tom, I don't suspect anyone, not really. I'm looking for reasons *not* to think it was someone in the family."

We finished our coffee and left. Since we had a little time before the family conference was to begin, we walked around the harbor and watched the Chappaquiddick ferry leaving. Edgartown was pretty in the twilight, quiet and serene. We leaned our elbows on a railing running along one of the piers and looked at the fading sunlight on the water. The mainland was only seven miles away, but we could have been in an alternate world. Tom finally broke the silence by saying, "Can you really believe that a Decker would kill another Decker? I could believe in magic before I could believe that. They're just too close-knit, Gillian."

"You said 'they.' Do you already consider yourself outside the family?"

He sighed. "I never was a Decker, at least not a very good one. I only married one, like you. And now that's ended. I spent nearly twenty years trying to play their game. That's long enough."

Twenty years. "I'm sorry, Tom."

"So am I, but for another reason. I should have broken off with the Deckers long ago, the way you did. But they are fascinating people, in their own way, aren't they? And there was another reason I couldn't do what you did."

I could guess. "Ike."

He nodded. "Ike. But now he's gone, and there's no real reason for me to stay any longer." He smiled at me. "You seem to have built a satisfying life for yourself without the Deckers. It's time I did the same.''

I didn't know how satisfying my life was, but I could think of another reason why it had been easier for me to break away than Tom: my husband was dead, while his wife was very much alive. Also, I hadn't spent anything like twenty years in the bosom of the family, as Tom had. The break was bound to be more traumatic for him than it'd been for me.

The sun was almost gone; I was thinking it was time for us to be going when Tom said, ''Don't go back to Chicago tomorrow. Take care of your business by phone and stay a little longer. We may never see each other again after this summer.''

I wouldn't mind seeing Tom again, since, as he said, he'd never been a very good Decker. ''Oh, Tom, we'll see each other.''

He gave me that sad smile I'd seen so much of lately. ''That's doubtful, don't you think? You'll be in Chicago and I'll be in Boston. I don't want to lose track of you again, Gillian. Not now. Stay.''

I didn't know what to say, so I retreated into silence. Tom put his arm around my shoulders and led me back toward the car. It was an intimate way to be walking, almost uncomfortably so. I could feel his body heat against my left arm, and I realized I'd never before thought of Tom so much as an individual, exclusive and unique to himself; before I'd seen only Annette's husband.

That was a mistake I intended not to repeat.

TWELVE

WHEN WE'D GATHERED at the Fergusons' at nine, I was in for a surprise: I met a third Connie Decker there. Connie the Mutable. The first Connie had been the quiet, placid woman content to live her life through her husband and her son. The second was the distraught and depressed Connie who'd lost the two people dearest to her and who needed pills to get through the day. But this Connie, Connie No. 3, was bubbling over with energy and news of what she and Mrs. Vernon had accomplished in their war against McDonald's. It was a time of changes indeed; that little old lady in the denim skirt and white sneakers had worked wonders.

"We decided not to bother with petitions," Connie told me. "This battle's going to be fought in the courts. We're talking to people about passing new and more stringent local ordinances—if we can blanket the island quickly, there won't be any spot of land where Big Mac can legally set up shop. We spent the day in Oak Bluffs, and tomorrow we're going to Edgartown, and—"

"And the day after to Chilmark," Joel said with a grin, "where both Auntie Connie and Mrs. Vernon will strip themselves nekkid when they carry their campaign to Lucy Vincent."

Lucy Vincent was a nude beach. Connie laughed and blushed, the only middle-aged woman I knew who could get away with that. "Actually, someone else is covering the upisland communities. Mrs. Vernon and I have all we can handle here. Tom, you promised me your help."

"You got it," he said. "Just don't send me up to Chilmark."

For some reason *up* on Martha's Vineyard was vaguely southwest; *down* was northeast. And to add to the fun, *down* was "in" while *up* was "out." West Chop, on the northernmost tip of the island, was elitist and private and for the most part pretended not to know the rest of the island was inhabited. Connie and Mrs. Vernon's venturing into alien territory to fight a hamburger franchise was undoubtedly considered puzzling, bizarre, and simply *not done*.

"You don't want to bother with Chilmark anyway," Michelle drawled. "There's nothing up there except psychiatrists."

Rob hadn't arrived yet; Michelle said he'd gotten a phone call just as they were leaving. Joel's being there was a surprise; family conferences in the past hadn't included the children. But he was almost a young man, and Michelle had told me he'd grown up fast...when Bobby died. Joel was a puzzle. He'd lost his brother and two cousins, playmates he'd grown up with, yet he was going about his life, windsurfing and having fun, as if he were unaffected by their loss. And I knew that couldn't be true.

Elinor was fighting a cold; she sat quietly in a corner and didn't have much to say. This was Oscar's meeting anyway; he kept the talk light and general, waiting for Rob to get there. Michelle looked tuned-out, in her elegant soft white floor-length dress; it dawned on me that I hadn't seen her in anything but white since we came to the Vineyard—her entire summer wardrobe was white. Tom had the fidgets, Connie was thinking about her own campaign instead of Oscar's, and I didn't really belong there. Their including me in the conference assumed too much: that I would be around to see the consequences of the decisions made that night.

Oscar was saying maybe they'd better start without Rob when Rob himself came bursting in. He'd evidently run all the way over because he was gulping in air in deep gasps. And his eyes were glittering; I'd never seen him so animated.

"They've caught him," he said, his voice hoarse with excitement. "The police have the killer in custody!"

Dead silence; we froze into a tableau of astonishment and disbelief. The only sound in the room was Rob's labored breathing. Then Elinor sneezed and broke the spell, and everyone started talking at once. *Who is he* and *Which police* and Connie's high voice saying *Are you sure are you sure*?

Rob gestured for silence. He took a deep breath and read from a piece of paper he'd brought with him; his hand was trembling. "That was Lowenstein on the phone. He—"

"Who?" Connie and I asked together.

"One of our private investigators," Michelle said.

"He said they'd been checking on people who'd been released from mental institutions around six months ago," Rob went on, "people with a history of violence. They've been searching these people's homes—yes, illegally—looking for anything that would tie them to us. Finally they hit pay dirt. A man named Matthew Zeitz—any of you ever heard the name?"

No one had.

"Well, this Zeitz is an electronics engineer who thinks his genius has never been properly appreciated. He's a bitter, violent man who almost killed his wife and who went berserk in his office and tried to kill his boss. He underwent treatment for a while and now is working again—different office. And evidently all is peaceful on the home front. Lowenstein thinks he picked us as a substitute target for his hostility... because we have the money and the recognition that have eluded him. Also, it would be safe to attack us since we don't know him."

"Are you sure he's the right man?" Connie asked.

"No question of it, Connie. When Lowenstein searched his house, he found boxes full of newspapers and magazine clippings about the family. He found photographs of all our houses, both here and on the mainland." He paused. "He even found snapshots of the kids, that Zeitz had taken himself. There are at least a dozen of Joel."

Joel sat very still, his face white.

"Lowenstein also found a list. All our names were on it—all but Gillian's. And four of the names had been crossed off." He paused a moment. "You know which ones, don't you? Bobby, Ike, Lynn, and Raymond. There's no doubt about it. This is the man.''

Oscar asked, ''How did the police get him? And where is this—Boston?''

Rob nodded. ''Boston. Lowenstein took a few of the photos and clippings and stuffed them in an envelope. He left the list behind. Then he went to the police.'' He consulted his piece of paper. ''To a Captain McCarthy. He told McCarthy he'd been following Zeitz when Zeitz left an envelope behind in a restaurant. The photos and clippings were enough for McCarthy to get a search warrant, and when they found the list . . . well. Zeitz flew into a rage and tried to strangle one of the police detectives—completely out of control, according to McCarthy. The arrest was made about an hour ago.''

Matthew Zeitz. All this agony had been caused by a nobody named Matthew Zeitz? A stranger. A lunatic. A Matthew Zeitz.

''I called Captain McCarthy,'' Rob continued. ''He says Zeitz will probably never go to trial because, in the captain's words, he's nutty as a fruitcake. Completely over the edge. Zeitz didn't even know his wife when she came to the police station.''

''What's going to happen?'' Michelle asked.

''Unofficially, McCarthy told me Zeitz would probably spend the rest of his life in a state mental institution. If he's ever declared legally sane, then he'll have to stand trial for murder. So . . .''

So it was safer to stay crazy.

''Then it's over,'' Tom breathed. ''It's really over!''

Everyone started talking again. We were all grinning at one another like a bunch of apes. A nervous, artificial laugh came from Joel; his mother frowned and the laughter stopped. Oscar announced, "This calls for a celebration! Time to break out the bubbly." He disappeared in the direction of the kitchen. Elinor sneezed and followed him.

Rob told us there wouldn't be any announcement of Zeitz's arrest in the news media; since his legal status was in the hands of state-appointed psychiatrists, the charge against him was only "suspicion"—of what, Captain McCarthy hadn't specified. But he'd agreed there was no need to make a big fuss about catching the Decker-killer until they were on more solid legal ground. So as far as the rest of the world was concerned, Raymond and the three kids all died in accidents.

Michelle nodded. "That's better for all of us."

"Absolutely," Tom agreed.

"How did you manage to talk him into that, Rob?" I asked. "Into keeping it out of the news?" His answer was lost in the general hubbub, perhaps on purpose.

"Well, at least that gets rid of Mom's objection," Joel said happily.

"Objection to what?" I asked him.

"To Uncle Oscar's running for the Senate."

Before I could ask him what he meant, Elinor and Oscar were back with two bottles of champagne and a tray of glasses. Oscar worked on the cork of the first bottle; it eased out with a sigh—no vulgar popping of corks in that house. The celebration was subdued, but there was no doubt that it was a celebration. Joel complained about not being allowed a second glass of champagne.

And yet, and yet... why didn't I feel relieved?

The rest of the evening passed in a blur. Whatever reservation Michelle had felt about Oscar's candidacy, it had disappeared with the news about Matthew Zeitz. They made plans, talked about people whose names meant nothing to me, drew up tentative timetables, made lists of contacts, talked strategy. Not one mention of issues or a platform. But even Connie made a couple of suggestions, surprising the others.

Something was wrong.

I sat and watched and listened, contributing nothing to the planning; it was if I were a one-person audience at a play. All the time they were talking politics, I was still thinking about the abrupt and unexpected end to the threat that had been hanging over the family all this time. The rest of them had taken the news, reacted to it, and now were getting on with their business. I was still reacting.

"Gillian, we're going to need your house, if you don't mind," Oscar said in his actor's voice he'd put on for the occasion. "My campaign manager and several of my aides will be descending upon us ere long," with a smile, "and we'll need a place to put them up." He was enjoying himself.

"Feel free," I answered vaguely.

"I think we'll move Nancy here," Elinor said. "Best to keep all the campaign people together."

During a lull I sought out Michelle. "Joel says you had an objection to Oscar's candidacy."

She looked annoyed. "Did he?"

Why was she annoyed? "Then you don't have any objection?"

"Of course not. Why should I?"

Nothing there. She was lying, obviously; I didn't even have to wonder about that. I waited a while and got Joel off away from the others. "Why didn't your mother want Oscar to run?"

"Aw, she just didn't want him to run right now. Too close to, you know, to what happened to Bobby and the others."

I nodded and let it go. Tom and Michelle were disagreeing on some point of strategy. Elinor excused herself to go take a pill. Oscar was pumping Rob for names of possible campaign contributors and Connie was asking questions every time anyone paused for breath. It wasn't until a good fifteen minutes had passed that the significance of what Joel had said hit me. I pleaded a headache and made my escape, refusing Tom's offer to walk me home.

I DIDN'T GO BACK to the house but went down to the beach instead. A cool breeze was blowing, something I needed to counteract the effects of the champagne. I found a flat rock and sat down, trying to get it all straight in my head.

Oscar had told me he'd been on the brink of running for the Senate once before, but he'd abandoned the campaign because of Theo. That seemed wise; the negative publicity, the sheer tastelessness of campaigning in the wake of the kidnapping and murder—that alone would be enough to defeat him. So Oscar's political career had suffered a setback because three would-be terrorists whose names I didn't know had zeroed in on young Theo Decker as their yellow brick road to fame and fortune. Running for office under those circumstances would have been impossible.

But something I'd overlooked entirely: wasn't that exactly what Oscar was planning to do now? Four members of his family murdered, one of them his own daughter, and Oscar was ready to brave the campaign trails anyway? Why was it not all right for Oscar to run after Theo's death—but it *was* all right to run after the deaths of Lynn and the other three? If it had been bad after Theo's death, wasn't it *four times* as bad now? I might not ever have thought of that if Joel hadn't let it slip that Michelle had some reservations.

The only significant difference I could see was that as far as the world was concerned, Lynn and the three others had all died in accidents. Well, maybe that was all the distinction that was needed. Public opinion is bizarre; tragic accidents within a family generate a certain amount of sympathy, whether people know the family personally or not. But if a man running for public office should be identified as a member of a family of murder victims, then what would the public response be? An unambivalent thumbs-down, a shrinking away in distaste, a naked revulsion mixed liberally with guilt. Voters as well as Oscar's political cronies would all know they ought to feel sorry for him; and when they couldn't, that's when the guilt would start seeping in. Things would go from bad to worse: only supermen don't resent those who make them feel guilty. *What's going on in that family?* the

question would be. And: *What have they done?*
What's wrong with them? Suicide, political suicide.

What a secret to have to keep! Passing off murders
as accidents. I stood up and started walking aimlessly
down the beach. What a coldhearted bunch the
Deckers seemed to me then; I could never have con-
cealed the murder of my child, no matter how worthy
the cause. But there was no point in putting all the
blame on Oscar; Elinor made most of his decisions for
him. Besides, they were all in it equally.

In a way, you could argue that the murders *were*
accidents. It was sheer accident that that madman
Matthew Zeitz picked out the Decker family as his
personal whipping-boy. Any prominent, well-to-do
family based in Boston would have fit the bill; it was
just the Deckers' bad fortune that Zeitz had settled on
them. But his arrest had come at exactly the right time;
now the story about "accidents" could be dissemi-
nated without fear of contradiction by further murders. It was all very convenient.

Just a little too damned convenient.

This is where it got hairy. Oscar had decided (that
is, Elinor had decided) to announce his candidacy
presumably on the basis that the trouble was over. But
that decision had been made *before* Rob rushed in
with the news that Matthew Zeitz had been arrested.
How had Oscar and Elinor known it was safe to go
ahead? Wasn't that taking an awful chance?

It occurred to me it wouldn't hurt to talk to this police captain in Boston myself. Rob had mentioned his
name several times—what was it? I waited. It came to
me: McCarthy. I glanced up at the house overlooking

the part of the beach I'd wandered to. It was Tom's; he was still at the Fergusons'. I climbed up the steps to the house and let myself in.

I found a phone and put in the call to Boston police headquarters. When I got through, I identified myself as Gillian Decker and asked to speak to Captain McCarthy.

It wouldn't have surprised me to hear he wasn't available or had gone home or something like that, but I was in no way prepared to learn there was no Captain McCarthy on the Boston police force. A patrolman by that name, a rookie, but no *Captain* McCarthy.

All right, then, Rob got the name wrong. I asked to speak to one of the arresting officers in the Matthew Zeitz case.

Shock number two. Matthew who?

My mouth had turned dry as the Sahara and I had to swallow a couple of times before I could speak. There can't be a whole lot of different ways of spelling "Zeitz" but I tried them all. Nobody by that name on the blotter. But he was arrested only a couple of hours ago, I insisted. No, lady, nobody here by that name. Well, a similar name? Nope. Nobody in the last two hours except a car thief, a small-time pusher, and a couple of drunk-and-disorderlies. I persisted until the desk sergeant started to lose patience; I thanked him and hung up.

No Captain McCarthy. No Matthew Zeitz. The whole stinking rotten story had been a lie.

I found the nearest bathroom and lost my dinner.

FOR A LONG TIME I sat on the bathroom floor and rested my head back against the wall. Why? Why in god's name had they done it? All along I'd felt something was wrong; on some level I'd recognized that I was watching acting, that I was an audience of one.

An audience of one? Delusions of grandeur. The show they'd put on must surely have been for Connie's benefit as well. And Joel's...maybe. Joel was still an enigma; I didn't know where he fit into all this.

But why tonight, on Oscar's big decision-making day? What had happened to prompt them to stage their little play at just this moment? Only one thing that I could see might have spurred them into it: I'd said I was going home. They'd tried to talk me into staying, into letting myself be absorbed back into the family. But when that didn't work—they'd determined to send me home thinking everything was peachy-keen in the Decker clan. I must have been asking too many questions, if they felt so strong a need to shut me up.

And so *The Rise and Fall of Matthew Zeitz*, tragicomedy in one act, was hurriedly staged for my elucidation and appeasement. The author? Rob Kurland, for one; Michelle was undoubtedly a co-author. But what of the others—were they in on it too? Elinor? Tom? Oscar? Did they know what was coming? Of course they knew; the only one I was sure had not been acting was Connie.

The only reason they would be going to such extremes was that they knew there'd be no more killings. I'd always felt they were too lacking in caution concerning their own safety—but now it made sense.

They knew the danger was over...that *had* to be it. They were protecting one of themselves.

But *that* didn't make sense! Which one could it be? Would Rob and Michelle have killed their own child? Michelle's grief over Bobby's death had been genuine, I was sure; and Rob was the only one in the family who'd named his first-born after himself. So what about Oscar and Elinor? Or Tom and Annette? Absurd. Connie Decker was the one truly innocent soul I knew on the face of the earth, but she was the only one left. I was back to Connie again. No, wait—there was one more.

Joel.

It all comes down to Joel—I'd heard that sentence more than once since I came back. I'd assumed it meant he was the last one left of the younger generation, but what if it had a more sinister meaning? I thought of the picture of the four kids Raymond had taken the summer before, the picture now resting on the mantelpiece in my room at Connie's house. The four kids laughing, touching one another, at ease together. How true a picture was it? I knew nothing of the way the four of them got along; all I knew was that Joel was the youngest, traditionally the tagalong spot. Did he feel overshadowed by the others? Bobby, the golden boy, destined to take over the family business. Lynn, already started in a political career and a swimming champion to boot. Ike, the genius, the one most likely to make the history books. And what did Joel do? He windsurfed.

It was hard to realize I was sitting on someone else's bathroom floor thinking my fifteen-year-old nephew was a murderer. I started feeling sick again. Was Joel capable of that much envy and hatred? And the adults—they were *accepting* what had happened, in order to keep alive their one remaining hope for continuing the family line? I bent over the toilet bowl again.

I don't know how long I'd been going at it before Tom came in and found me. He gave me a glass of diluted mouthwash to rinse out the bad taste and helped me to my feet. Then he led me to a sofa and told me to lie down; he stacked a couple of cushions for me to put my feet up on. A moment later I felt a cool damp cloth on my forehead. Then Tom handed me something to drink; it was chalky and tasted terrible, but it did calm my stomach. Nothing like having a cardiac surgeon on hand to treat a case of nausea.

Tom looked worried. "What's wrong, Gillian? What caused this?"

I couldn't tell him; he was one of *them*. God, how I hated the Deckers and all the people they'd married! I wanted to get away from here, away from these awful people and their ugly murders! I was going to be on the first plane out tomorrow morning.

That's right, Gillian. Run away. As you always do.

I could feel tears welling up in my eyes; it had been years since I'd last cried, but I couldn't seem to stop now. Tom sat quietly on the sofa by me, holding my hand and saying nothing, waiting. I turned my head away from him.

Oh, how I wanted to be back in my own house in Chicago! But as I gradually calmed down and the tears stopped, I admitted against my will that escape was not really possible. No matter how fast I ran or how far, I'd still be carrying the Decker problem with me. When I'd run away before, I'd thought I could make the Deckers one episode in my life, over and done with once I left. That must surely have been the most naive assumption of my life.

No, once you were exposed to the Deckers, they had you. They had you for life. Even if I moved to a mountain top in Tibet, the Deckers would be there with me. And how could I spend the rest of my life not knowing the truth of what was happening now? I couldn't go home yet; as much as I wanted to get away, I couldn't leave this problem behind me. If I was right about Joel, I didn't know what I could do about it. But I had to see it through. No running away this time.

"Are you feeling better?" Tom asked.

"Yes, a little."

I struggled to sit up, but Tom gently pushed me back down, telling me to wait a while. "Give yourself time. Gillian, can't you talk about it?"

"No, I can't." Not to you, Dr. Tom Henry, married to a high-style, manipulative, twinny-type Decker. Married . . . but divorcing. Was it possible he'd been excluded from tonight's little exercise in the dramatic arts? Perhaps he didn't even know about Joel. Oh, get real, Gillian! It was more likely I just wanted Tom to be innocent of all guilty knowledge, because I liked him. Hell, I didn't know; I was in no condition to make decisions or even distinguish what was true from what wasn't. Joel a fifteen-year-old killer? He'd have to be insane. I was beginning to feel a little nutty myself.

After a while I sat up and apologized to Tom. "Not the nicest thing to come home to—a near-stranger vomiting in your bathroom."

He smiled. "Hardly a stranger. I felt I'd gotten to know you, Gillian—but obviously I missed something important. Won't you tell me what's upset you so much?"

Instead of answering I got up and wandered about the room. Annette had decorated it; her taste was everywhere. I picked up a Legras glass vase of a rare red ground color; the internal decoration showed three birds in cameo endlessly circling the body of the vase. I never wanted to break anything so much in my life.

But I put the vase back down. I was in over my head and I needed to talk to someone . . . yet as much as I liked Tom, I couldn't bring myself to trust him. Not completely. I wanted to, but I couldn't.

I looked at him sitting on the sofa, watching me. His face was troubled, and it was troubled on my account. He wanted to help and I wouldn't let him. God, had I become so suspicious and untrusting that I couldn't recognize good intent when I saw it?

"Tom, I want to stay here with you tonight," I told him flatly.

He gave me no argument.

THIRTEEN

TOM WAS STILL ASLEEP when I left the following morning. It was barely light out, and Connie was still in her room when I slipped into the house. I showered and changed and was in the kitchen squeezing oranges by the time she came down.

"How's your headache?" she greeted me.

"Completely gone," I said with a smile.

"That's good. Your door was closed when I got home last night and I didn't want to bother you. I'm glad you're feeling better."

I *was* feeling better, a lot. Nothing had changed, but a night of strenuous lovemaking had been just what I needed to give me the backbone to see this problem through to the end. I hadn't told Tom I knew the Matthew Zeitz story was a phony, because I still hadn't figured out the degree of his complicity in the deception or even whether he was involved at all or not. All I'd wanted from Tom was the comfort of a warm body wrapped around mine. He could be an ally, but I didn't dare risk telling him what I knew just yet. For the time being, I was willing to settle for the mere illusion that someone was *on my side*.

Tom was a good lover, and I was fond of him; so I felt a little guilty about using him to satisfy an immediate need. Also, I had to wonder about what was happening to me, to my common sense. Going to bed with a man I couldn't quite bring myself to trust—that was something new. But it was hard to maintain any sort of perspective in the atmosphere of deceit and conspiracy the Deckers had generated; I couldn't rely on my own judgment anymore. I thought I knew these people, but I didn't, not really. The only one in the entire crowd I felt I could trust was Connie.

Right then she was talking about Matthew Zeitz; she'd accepted the story without question. Connie wondered how he could have been tracking them all this time without anyone's noticing. "I don't understand what makes people do things like that! He didn't even know us. What was he thinking? What went so wrong in his life that he started . . . killing people?"

Connie really was a sweet woman. Here she was talking about a man she thought had killed her husband, and she had enough compassion to spare a thought about what had happened to *him*. "Something traumatic had to have happened," I said, going along. "Something so awful that it warped him completely."

"I wonder what it was," she murmured.

Don't waste your sympathy, I wanted to tell her; *Matthew Zeitz doesn't exist*. I took my orange juice and went to stand by the one kitchen window that looked out on the ocean. The sunlight on the water was already a burning glare; today was going to be a hot one.

Connie changed the subject. "Gillian, do you really have to go back to Chicago today? Couldn't you—"

"I've decided to stay on," I told her. "My assistant can handle the auction."

Her face lit up. "Oh, I'm so glad! That's wonderful, Gillian!" She really did look pleased, and that made me smile too. "You belong here, you know." She stopped to clear her throat. "Mrs. Vernon and I have a meeting in Edgartown today. With people from the other communities who're going to help fight the franchise?"

"Yes?"

"Michelle and Rob and Elinor and Tom are all coming—Oscar can't make it, his people from Washington are getting in today." She paused and then asked wistfully, "I don't suppose you'd like to come too, would you?"

Through the window I spotted Joel climbing the steps up from the beach. "I'd love to come," I told Connie.

That pleased her too. "The more Deckers there, the more chance we have of persuading other people to join in. That's what Mrs. Vernon says."

Bless Mrs. Vernon. Joel came bursting in in his usual uninhibited manner; he gave Connie a kiss and turned to me, sudden disappointment showing on his face. "You're not wearing your swim suit! Hey, Aunt Gillian—you don't want to miss going out today! Now that they've caught old Matthew Whatsisname, we don't have to stay in so close to shore anymore!"

"Zeitz," Connie said.

I could barely look at him, my most likely murderous teen-aged nephew. "No windsurfing for me today," I said. "I'm going to a meeting with Connie."

"That's right, Joel," she said. "This morning. You can go surfing another time."

"Righty-o." He shrugged. "Are you really going back to Chicago?"

"Not right away. My business there can take care of itself."

"Terrif!" He swooped me up in a big hug; I pushed away quickly. Joel hesitated. "Aunt Gillian, are you mad at me or something?"

Oh dear. "Why should I be mad?"

"I dunno. But you seem, well, like you're mad."

I forced myself to look straight at him...and all I saw was the puzzled face of a fifteen-year-old, poised midway between childhood and adulthood, wondering whether he was reading his grown-up aunt correctly or not. "No, Joel, I'm not mad. I'm a little preoccupied today, that's all. This just isn't a good time for me to be thinking about windsurfing."

His face broke into a relieved grin. "Sure. We'll go another time." He gave Connie a wink and was gone. I could hear him whistling as he clattered down the wooden steps to the beach.

THE MEETING WAS already in full swing by the time we arrived; Connie had got the time wrong. Tom was waiting by the door for us. He gave my arm a squeeze and whispered he was glad I wasn't leaving; I wondered if he thought I was staying because of him. Connie had insisted on calling the rest of the family with the news that I wouldn't be going back to Chicago for a while; they all knew, and probably construed from that that their Matthew Zeitz ploy had worked. Tom led us to where the rest of the Decker contingent was sitting.

We were meeting in a room of Edgartown's yacht club, and it was crowded. At the front of the room three of the island's lawyers were arguing strategy, with Mrs. Vernon interrupting them every other sentence. The rest of the group wasn't exactly quiet either; everyone had a question to ask or a suggestion to make or an opinion to express. It was every bit as bad as I'd thought it would be.

Elinor hadn't come; her cold had got the better of her. So she'd sent Nancy Younger in her place, to be seen but not heard, to help swell the ranks of Deckers there to endorse the island-wide war against McDonald's. I sat next to Nancy, who even on this hot day was dressed like a graduate of Miss Finicky's Finishing School, right down to the mandatory single strand of pearls. Michelle flashed me a quick smile ... *oh, how one may smile, and smile, and be a villain*. Rob was on his feet arguing with somebody.

Then I took a good look at the somebody—and I recognized him. It was the man who'd come over to our table at the Bay Tower Room in Boston, the day Annette had taken Connie and me shopping. He was the one who owned cable TV and radio stations.

I leaned over to Nancy. "That man who's arguing with Rob—who is he?"

"Ah...that's Mr. Underwood," she said in her usual whisper.

Underwood—that's right, I remembered. "Patrick?"

She said yes. I was glad to see him again; I recalled he'd seen a play I had directed in New York, and that made him kind of rare. The meeting dragged on, getting nowhere. Nancy kept leaning around me to say things to Tom, who answered her in barely polite monosyllables. Mrs. Vernon was angry at one of the lawyers, who was angry at Patrick Underwood, who was angry at Rob.

Finally Michelle stood up. "May I say something?" she asked in her meticulous, I'm-used-to-being-listened-to manner of speaking. Every head in the room swiveled toward her; one of the lawyers invited her to the front of the room with a gesture. She walked to the front languidly, taking her time, enjoying being the center of attention.

For she *was* the center of all attention in that room. She looked fantastic, with her off-the-shoulder white dress and her glistening, short black hair and her red, red mouth. It wasn't just the men who were looking, either; the women liked watching her too. Michelle faced the rest of the room with a half smile playing about her lips and struck her favorite pose—hand on hip, foot forward.

"We're not going to get anywhere talking at cross-purposes like this," she said. "We ought to be following the same rules of order as any other meeting— no one speaks unless recognized, and we stick to one topic at a time. This meeting needs a chairman."

In no time at all Michelle was installed as chair, and from that point on the meeting proceeded in an orderly manner. When they started on the subject of what legal steps they could take to make sure that no public land was leased to McDonald's, I tuned out. I just couldn't get all worked up about hamburgers right then.

Eventually the meeting came to an end and I was on my feet immediately; I'd been sitting too long. I looked around to see Patrick Underwood heading in my direction.

"Gillian! I thought that was you," he said, smiling. So he remembered my name. "Aren't you glad you came here for the summer? Think of all the excitement you'd have missed."

I smiled back. "I *am* thinking of it."

"How'd you get roped in on the franchise fight? Connie?"

"Yep, Connie. It was either this meeting or go windsurfing with Joel."

His eyebrow went up. "I'd like to see you on a surfboard. But I think we can come up with better options than that. Are you busy tonight? Why don't we—"

"Hello, Patrick," Tom interrupted, "good to see you again." The two men shook hands. "I didn't know you knew Gillian."

"We've met, in Boston. I think it was the Bay Tower Room, wasn't it, Gillian? Annette introduced us." Did I imagine it, or was there a slight emphasis on the name of Tom's wife?

"Just recently, then?"

"Yes. I was about to ask Gillian to have dinner with me tonight."

Tom casually draped an arm around my waist. *Claiming* me. "Gillian's busy tonight."

The look on Patrick's face said he got the message, but he didn't back off. "Tomorrow, then?"

Tom's fingers pressed against my side, signaling me. "I'm afraid Gillian's pretty much tied up for the rest of her stay here. I'm sure you can find another dinner companion."

Patrick looked at Tom coolly and said, "I'd like to hear her say that."

That was my cue. "It's true, Patrick. I'm . . . tied up."

Tom relaxed his hold on my waist and let out a barely audible breath. He'd won. He smiled at Patrick with a new affability and asked, "Hasn't Mrs. Vernon snared you for one of her committees yet?"

"Not yet, although I'll be happy to do what I can."

"That's good to hear." He called Mrs. Vernon over. "We have a volunteer for you."

She gave us a toothy grin. "Ah, Patrick, I'd been meaning to get to you. You have friends in Chilmark, haven't you?"

"Yes, several. What have you got in mind?"

"What I've got in mind is getting those hedonists up off their naked behinds and *organized*. That's where you and Tom come in."

"Me?" Tom said, surprised.

"Both of you." Mrs. Vernon gave me her disconcertingly direct stare. "Gillian, I'm going to have to take them away from you. D'you mind?"

Would it matter if I did? "No, of course not—go ahead." Both Tom and Patrick threw me a rueful look and followed the small woman in the denim skirt and white sneakers.

He was jealous! Tom was jealous! Or pretending to be. Whoa, now—*pretending* to be jealous? Good god, what was the matter with me? Wasn't I going to trust anyone's motives ever again?

Connie was gathered into Mrs. Vernon's little group, and Michelle and Rob were heading back to West Chop to play tennis. I declined their offer of a lift and invited Nancy Younger to have lunch with me.

WE FOUND A PLACE right on the Edgartown waterfront. I ordered the "Tourist's Special" (which tourist? I wondered)—fried clams and cole slaw. Nancy asked for a salad.

The food came and we dug in. Well, *I* dug in; Nancy chewed every bite precisely thirteen times. (Yes, I counted.) After thirty-nine chews and three swallows, she patted her mouth with a napkin and said in a voice so faint I could barely hear her, "You and Tom are very close, aren't you?"

Oh-oh. "The last time I saw Tom Henry was ten years ago. We didn't keep in touch."

She stared at her salad and wouldn't meet my eyes. "He didn't want you to have dinner with Mr. Underwood."

So she'd heard that, had she? I looked at her, her eyes still fixed on her salad plate. Nancy's bad case of puppy love for a not-interested married man couldn't be making her very happy. She must have been in seventh heaven when Tom and Annette decided to divorce, but surely she understood by now that Tom wasn't going to turn to her. Yet, hope does have a way of springing eternal... I settled on a kind lie. "Tom doesn't like Patrick Underwood, and don't ask me why—I don't know. I just know Tom doesn't want the family to have anything to do with him.''

Slowly she raised her eyes from her plate. "Oh. Then ... then you and Tom aren't ... ?''

I pretended to be shocked. "Of course not! Why, he's still married to Annette!'' God, what a hypocrite.

Nancy looked embarrassed and relieved at the same time and whispered an apology. We changed the subject and that was that.

I bit down on something nicely crunchy; the cole slaw had jicama in it. Nancy talked about what she and Elinor were working on and speculated on new directions the Decker Philanthropic Foundation might take. Elinor was thinking of expanding the fields of endeavor she usually funded. "It'll mean a lot more work for her,'' Nancy said, "but personally I think that would be a good thing. It'll help take her mind off Lynn.''

"Does she dwell on what happened, do you think?''

She thought about that a moment. "I don't think so, but Elinor doesn't confide in me about personal matters. When Lynn died, she just sort of withdrew from everybody for a while. Grieving in private, I guess. Coming so soon after the deaths of Ike Henry and Bobby Kurland—well, it was hard.''

I nodded. "They've all lost a child. Starting with Connie, four years ago.''

"Oh yes, wasn't that a *dreadful* thing! That poor boy. I hadn't been working for Elinor very long when

Theo was kidnapped, but I could see it was just tearing the family apart. It was all anyone talked about.''

"Did you know Theo Decker at all? How soon after you started working for Elinor was he killed?''

"About six months, but I did meet him once—here on the island, in fact. It was right before they left for Norway. Theo was a nice boy—I liked him. I was so sorry when they couldn't get all the money together. I'd have given them my own if I'd had any.''

I wasn't sure I'd heard her right. "What do you mean, they couldn't get all the money together?''

She looked at me in surprise. "Raymond was able to pay only part of the ransom—you didn't know?''

"I've been gone, remember. There was nothing about that in the paper.''

"Wasn't there? Well, no, I suppose there wouldn't be. But the kidnappers wanted this horrendous sum of money, and they didn't give the family much time to raise it—not enough to convert stock holdings into cash, or some such. Anyway, Raymond paid what he could, but they went ahead and killed Theo anyway. You'd think they'd wait for the rest, wouldn't you?''

This was incomprehensible. "But couldn't Raymond get a bank loan on his securities? And what about the rest of the family—didn't they help?''

"Yes indeed, everybody helped. Elinor had me going through the Foundation budget to see how much cash we could divert. I don't think that was strictly legal,'' Nancy said softly, "but we did it anyway. Almost a million dollars of Foundation money went toward Theo's ransom. I don't know about any bank loans.''

I questioned her some more, but Nancy had told me all she knew. When the cards were down, the rich, affluent, well-to-do, moneyed, wealthy, *loaded* Deckers couldn't come up with enough cash to save one of their own. I didn't believe it. The newspaper account of Raymond's death had said that the firm of Decker and Kurland was worth an estimated $600 million. The kidnappers had wanted only twenty (only!)—so Raymond should have had no trouble paying them off. Unless the newspaper figure was inflated. This needed looking into.

Nancy had driven Elinor's Rolls to the meeting in Edgartown, and I rode back with her. She was uneasy about driving the expensive car and never took her eyes off the road; we crept along the federal secondary highway like two octogenerians whose chauffeur had just quit. Conversation would obviously be a dangerous distraction, so I kept silent.

I kept silent and thought about Tom. I didn't like the way he'd moved in when Patrick Underwood was asking me out to dinner. Not that I was panting for a date with Patrick, although that might be nice—but it was just too damned possessive of Tom, too presumptuous. What had happened between us was too quick and too recent for either one of us to be staking a claim, not to mention the legal nicety of Tom's still being married to another woman. His cutting Patrick out like that was way out of line; I'd gone along with it just to avoid a scene. No—I'd gone along because I was chicken; I was so unsure of everybody around me that I'd simply taken the path of least resistance.

Damn Tom anyway! What right did he have putting me in a position like that?

Then it occurred to me that I might be looking for excuses to see Tom in an unfavorable light . . . to justify my continuing reluctance to trust him. What if I simply went up to him and said, *I know that the Matthew Zeitz story is bullshit*—what would he do? Try to convince me it wasn't? Claim he didn't know anything about it? I wasn't quite ready to put it to the test.

When we reached West Chop, I asked Nancy to drop me at the tennis club. I had to see the Kurlands.

MICHELLE AND ROB were in a doubles match with a couple I didn't know. A ball boy hovered on the sidelines, eager to earn a big tip. The Kurlands and their two opponents all played well. It wasn't the high-powered game of younger players—no lethal serves, no killer overhead smashes. Instead, their game was one of grace and finesse; at any other time it would have been a pleasure to watch them. Michelle's tennis dress was so white that the glare hurt my eyes.

Finally Rob served out the set and they took a break. Rob was the first to spot me. "Hello, Gillian! Glad you're here. We didn't get a chance to tell you at the meeting, but we're delighted you decided to stay on for a while."

Are you, now. "Yes, my business can take care of itself. I was getting antsy over nothing."

"Good, good. You deserve a real vacation—after all the family trouble you walked in on. But that's over now. The best thing we can do is forget about it."

"I suppose you're right." *Liar, liar.*

"Michelle and I are taking the sailboat out tomorrow. Why don't you come along?"

I mumbled a hasty acceptance and started to ask him a question, but the male half of the couple they were playing came up to us just then. He acknowledged the introduction Rob made and immediately started talking about some upcoming tennis tournament. I eased away and went over to sit down on a bench where Michelle was toweling off.

"Ah, Gillian," she said. "Connie called us with the good news. I think you're right to stay."

Yes, yes—enough of these amenities. "Michelle, are you having money problems?"

She put down the towel and picked up a thermos. "We're in the money-problems business."

"I mean, do you have enough money?"

"Does anyone ever have enough money?" she said with a laugh.

"Michelle. Serious question."

My tone of voice must have convinced her. She poured herself a cold drink and offered me one; I shook my head. "Yes, I can see it is," she said, sipping her drink. "No, I'm not having money problems."

"The business isn't in trouble?"

"The business is doing fine. Why do you ask?"

"What about four years ago? Was it in trouble then?"

She frowned. "Gillian, Decker and Kurland hasn't been in serious trouble in all the time I've been with the firm. What's this all about?"

I took a deep breath and said, "Raymond's obituary notice reported the firm's assets to be in the neighborhood of six hundred million. Is that an accurate figure?"

"Fairly accurate. A little more right now."

"Then will you please tell me why in the name of heaven you weren't able to come up with twenty million to buy Theo Decker's life?"

I'd never seen her look so dismayed. "Oh, Gillian, it's not that simple! We don't have huge sums of money lying about that we can put our hands on anytime we like. We—" She was interrupted by the female half of the other couple, summoning everyone back to the court. Michelle gave an exasperated laugh and said, "Your sense of timing is not the best I've seen. We'll talk later—not here." We both stood up. "Rob and I are taking a new sailboat out tomorrow—"

"I know. I'm coming."

"Fine. We'll talk then." I started to leave. "Where are you going?" Michelle asked.

"To Connie's."

"Do you have transportation?"

Oh lord—I hadn't thought of that. "I'll walk."

"Nonsense, it's way too far. And in this sun? You'll get heatstroke."

"What about you—out there playing tennis?"

She ignored me. "Let's see—I think the Mattinglys just finished their match." She sent the ball boy with a message, and I had a ride home. Michelle didn't care for the unseemly notion of my walking all the way back to the Decker compound and therefore I would not walk. Was it a kindness on her part or just a chance to arrange things to her own liking? Michelle did so like arranging things.

The Mattinglys turned out to be a middle-aged couple with skin like leather, both of them. They talked tennis all the way to the compound, assuming I was as fascinated by the game as they were. Nothing more was required of me than to smile and nod and say *Ah!* in the right places. I thanked them politely for the lift.

FOURTEEN

ANNETTE WAS BACK.

She'd scored a triumph in Paris. The proposed software distributorship was safely under legal lock and key, and the personnel problems had been resolved to her satisfaction; she'd gotten rid of three of the four young men whose business she was putting Decker money into. Jules—the "obsessed" one—had been reluctant to cut his friends and partners out, so Annette had taken matters into her own hands.

"I bought them off," she said cheerfully. "That's all they were in it for anyway, a quick payoff. Jules was *crushed*. He's such an innocent, he'd had no idea his so-called friends were riding on his coattails."

"It sounds as if Jules could use a babysitter," Michelle remarked.

"I've already found him one," Annette said. "Do you remember Louis Benoit? He worked on the French telephone system ..." And the twins were off into the world of business.

Annette looked vibrant; her trip had done her good. It was the first time I'd seen the twins together since Raymond's funeral, and I'd forgotten how overwhelming the two of them could be side by side. Annette's bright red dress made a dramatic contrast to Michelle's all-white outfit; you couldn't ignore those two if your life depended on it.

Tom's immediate reaction to Annette's return was to ask Connie if he could move into one of her spare rooms. My house was rapidly filling up with Oscar's campaign staff, a few of whom would be staying in the Ferguson house along with Nancy Younger. Connie said yes, of course. I wasn't sure how I felt about Tom's moving in with us. It would be convenient having him right down the hall from me—oh my, yes. And, yes, a little bit exciting as well. On the other hand, if Tom turned out to be in cahoots with Rob and whoever else was in on the Matthew Zeitz lie, I didn't want him close to me at all.

I couldn't even rule out Annette's being in on it; a little thing like an ocean wasn't enough to isolate her from what was going on here on Martha's Vineyard. She'd probably stayed in daily contact with her twin and must know more of what was happening than I did. But that was only a side issue, the Matthew Zeitz business; it told me I couldn't trust anybody. But it wasn't the real problem; the real problem was Joel. What was to be done about Joel?

The authority figures in his life were handling it all wrong, pretending as they were that life would go on as usual if they were just nice to Joel and protected him against outside harassment. But surely if he'd killed before and got away with it, he'd kill again. What kind of psychosis always showed itself by age fifteen—paranoid schizophrenia, or was I thinking of something else? If there was any hope of helping him, he had to get that help *now*; later might not do any good.

I was muddling all this over while I helped Tom move in that evening. "Did you bring your gun?"

He hesitated, and then said, "Yes. Does that bother you?"

"I don't know why you need it, now that they've caught Matthew Zeitz."

"Habit, mostly. I'll get rid of it if you like."

I shrugged and decided to take a mini-chance. "Do you believe Rob's story about that man?"

"Matthew Zeitz? Well, yes . . . is there some reason I shouldn't?"

"None that I can think of. It does seem rather fortuitous, though. All of a sudden—bam! We gottim!"

"All of a sudden?" Tom sounded incredulous. "It may be sudden for you, Gillian, but for us it's been dragging on for four months. Both the police and our private investigators have been looking for the man all that time, remember?"

"That wasn't exactly what I meant. I meant that the sudden emergence of a total stranger as the killer . . . well, it neatly defuses any suspicion that it might be a member of the family, doesn't it?"

Tom came over and took me by the shoulders. "Gillian—do you have doubts that Matthew Zeitz is the killer?"

I almost told him right then that I knew Joel had killed his son Ike and what's more *he* knew it. But I chickened out. "No, not really. It's just hard for me to maintain any perspective on all this."

He gave me a big hug; my arms slipped around his waist and I hugged him back. Tom was so warm and solid and concerned; I didn't want to let go. But one of us had a serious character flaw. Either Tom was every bit as untrustworthy as I feared he was, or else there was something wrong with me for not being able to trust.

He led me over to the bed, where he patted the mattress affectionately. "You're going to help me break this in, aren't you?"

I wouldn't have minded jumping into bed right then, but I said, "Better wait until Connie's gone."

The evening meal was a catch-as-catch-can affair. I made some iced coffee; Tom and Connie threw together a hasty salad; and after that it was every man for himself. I found some cheese and cold cuts in the fridge, while Tom put something frozen into the microwave. Connie barely ate a bite.

She was all atwitter; Mrs. Vernon had a meeting lined up for them in East Chop that evening, but what really had Connie excited was the coverage given their activities by the *Gazette*, the only newspaper on the island. "The front page, Gillian—look at that! And our picture, too!" Connie with her about-average height and gnomish Mrs. Vernon made a Mutt-and-Jeff pair; both wore suitably sober expressions.

"You look very serious," Tom said.

"We *are* very serious. Look what it says here. It says the fact that this time the battle against McDonald's is being led by two West Choppers shows exactly how serious the threat is."

That was true. West Chop itself didn't have to worry about a hamburger heaven appearing in its midst; the tennis club would never permit it. The tennis club—the very one where I'd stopped by to talk to Michelle—

acted as a sort of governing board for West Chop real estate; nobody bought land or built a new house without the tennis club's approval. West Chop normally did not involve itself in the affairs of the rest of the island; it was a private world inside the rest of Martha's Vineyard. West Chop was Bostonian; East Chop thought it was; Oak Bluffs was nightlife for the tourists; Edgartown was opera singers, newscasters, and movie stars. And writers lived all over the place. But two West Choppers emerging from their citadel of privilege in order to Save the Island was front-page news indeed.

As Connie chattered on, I watched her with wonder and pleasure. It was hard to believe that this was the same woman who not too long ago had complained so bitterly about newspapers and front-page photos. Of course, her privacy wasn't being invaded now, and that made all the difference. Connie truly was a changed woman, and I couldn't have been happier for her.

But my excuse for staying on was gone now; Connie didn't need me. Now I was staying because of Joel.

OUR LOVEMAKING was less frenetic than the first time; Tom was more relaxed and I wasn't fighting the screaming-meemies after having just learned the Matthew Zeitz story was a hoax, the way I'd been before. We were in my room, and we took our time. It was more like real *love*making this time.

After a while Tom got up and made us both a drink from the tray of necessaries we'd brought upstairs with us. He stopped and looked at the photograph of the four kids I had propped up on the mantelpiece. "Great picture. Who took it?"

"Raymond."

He picked it up and studied it closely. "It looks . . . lovingly taken."

"That's a surprise?"

He didn't answer but put the picture back and came to sit on the side of the bed, saying nothing. Unexpectedly coming across a picture of his dead son had shaken him. I pulled him down and kissed that place right between his eyes. "It's hard without him, isn't it?"

"Harder than I would ever have thought possible. I look at Joel running along the beach healthy and free and I . . ." He trailed off.

And you want to kill him. "Did Joel and Ike get along well?"

"Did they ever. You'd think they were brothers to see them together. Ike kind of liked playing big brother, since he was an only child. And Joel—well, Joel is everybody's kid brother."

"Didn't he ever feel left out?"

"Left out? Ike?"

"No, Joel. He was younger than the rest of them. Tagalongs usually end up feeling like outsiders."

Tom shook his head. "The only outsiders here are you and I." Then he laughed. "I doubt if Joel has any idea of what alienation is all about. He's been an insider all his life."

"Come on, Tom, he's an adolescent boy! He must be loaded with insecurities."

"You'd think so, wouldn't you?" he answered ambivalently.

This wasn't exactly the happy postcoital love talk I'd anticipated, but Tom had provided an opening I'd be a fool not to follow up. "How close was Joel to Theo Decker?"

Tom shrugged. "They were all close. They were a happy pack of kids, a closed circle. Too closed, I sometimes thought. They had other friends, but the five of them together were something special."

"So when Theo was killed..."

"The other four were devastated. It was their first contact with death, you see, and Theo was sort of their leader."

History was repeating itself in reverse; first the leader of the younger generation was murdered, then the leader of the older. Leaving a wake of resentment and grief in both instances. I took my courage in hand and said, "Tom, I just learned today that Raymond wasn't able to pay the entire amount of the ransom."

He nodded, said nothing.

"Why, Tom? Twenty million! Among all of you, you couldn't raise twenty million?"

No answer for a moment, and then he murmured, "'First, do no harm.'"

"What?"

He sighed, suddenly sounding very tired. "It's the opening line of the Hippocratic oath. 'First, do no harm.' At the time Theo was kidnapped, I was with a patient. I wasn't even at home, I was..." He smiled wryly as he remembered where he'd been. "I was in Chicago. I was inserting a new kind of valve into the heart of a twelve-year-old girl suffering from bacterial endocarditis...alpha streptococci had shrunk her own valve beyond repair. New technology, new procedure—very tricky. If I'd left the girl then, she could have died...and I would have killed her. I told Annette to do whatever was necessary to raise the money—we had each other's power of attorney. By the time I was able to get away, it was all over. Theo was dead."

I was silent a moment. "What happened to your patient?"

Tom smiled. "She's now a healthy, happy sixteen-year-old. I hear she plays basketball."

So he'd been able to save one of them. "How much money was Annette able to raise?"

"Only a couple of million. I'd thought it would be more."

So did I. "You said the other four kids were devastated by Theo's death—Joel too?"

"Joel especially. He loved Theo almost as much as his brother Bobby. Why do you keep asking about Joel?"

Careful. "Because he seems to have adjusted so well to the deaths of his brother and Ike and Lynn."

"This is bad?"

"No, but it is unusual, isn't it?"

"Well, he's four years older now. He was only eleven when Theo died."

"No survivor's guilt?"

"No sign of it. Joel has a healthy ego-structure. Good thing, too—did you know the Kurlands were changing their name?"

"No! To Decker?"

"A compromise. Decker-Kurland. But what do you want to bet the 'Kurland' part drops off before too many more years have passed?"

"Not one penny. Whoo, a semi-identity change on top of everything else. I don't think I could have handled all that at fifteen."

"Don't worry about Joel, Gillian. If he needs help, he'll get it."

I wondered if that was Tom's way of telling me to butt out. No, on second thought he probably meant exactly what he said: *Don't worry*. As far as Tom was concerned, it was over.

I wished I felt the same.

I SLIPPED OUT of the house early the next morning, in case Joel should get it into his head to show up as he'd done a couple of times before. I still hadn't figured out a way to talk to him or even look at him. If he was psychotic, he was *sick*, not evil. But it was hard to remember that whenever I thought of Bobby, Lynn, and Ike. And Raymond. Dear, protective Raymond, who'd died trying to save his nephew from himself. The trouble with that was that Joel didn't *act* sick. He acted like a kid, an ordinary kid. But . . . process of elimination. Would the adults protect one of themselves who had killed his or her own child? No. But they would conspire to protect Joel.

Oscar was in his kitchen creating an omelet; Elinor was still in bed nursing her cold, he said. "When you reach our age," he added, "little illnesses tend to hang on about four times as long as they used to. Have you had breakfast?"

I said no, and he cracked a couple more eggs over a bowl. I waited until he'd served the omelet (it was delicious) and asked, "What about Nancy and your campaign people? Don't they get any?"

"This morning they scrounge for themselves. We're flying our cook in from Washington this afternoon. She's going to have her hands full."

"Lots of people to cook for?"

"Only three of my aides so far, plus Elinor and me. And Nancy—almost forgot Nancy. But people will be coming and going for the rest of the summer."

I asked an impudent question. "Tell me, Oscar—do you look upon the Senate as your *ultima Thule* or is it only a stepping stone?"

"To the White House?" He laughed easily. "You know, Gillian, at one time I did have my eyes set on the Presidency. But that was a long time ago, and the country has changed considerably since then. For one thing, the world is no longer run by governments, it's run by corporations. Now I can have the most effect making the laws that restrain the corporations—or cooperate with them, whichever is better for the country in each case. No, I no longer want to be President. I'll have more real clout in the Senate than I would in the White House. The Presidency is almost as much show biz as it is executive power."

No wonder only mediocre men sought the office now. "Are you going to introduce any antiterrorist laws?"

He grimaced. "Laws can't do anything about terrorists without the muscle to back them up."

"So you just pay them off? Or *not* pay them off?"

Oscar regarded me coolly across his empty plate. "The tone of this conversation has suddenly taken a turn toward the decidedly unpleasant. What's bothering you, Gillian?"

"Theo is bothering me. The fact that the rest of you didn't help Raymond raise the total amount demanded by Theo's kidnappers."

He looked surprised. "But we did help!"

"Not much. Not enough."

"We were able to scrape together seventeen million, all of us together. That was only three shy."

"Yes, *only*. Only three million more to save Theo's life—and you couldn't come up with it?"

Anger flashed in his eyes. "Good god, Gillian—don't you understand? That boy was dead the minute those Asian hoodlums first laid their hands on him. If we'd paid them two hundred million, they'd still have killed him!"

I couldn't believe what I was hearing. "And so you decided that since there was no hope of saving him, why throw good money away? You all chipped in just enough to make Raymond think you were trying to help?"

Now he was really angry. "Who the hell do you think you are, Miss High-and-Mighty? You turn your back on us for ten years and then you come waltzing in here and start pronouncing moral judgment?"

I counted to ten and then said, "Oscar—I'm sorry. I know that's what it must look like. But I'm just trying to understand. Help me understand."

Politician-like, he regained his composure instantly. He got up and went over to lean against the kitchen counter where he could look down at me, still sitting at the table. "I've always felt it was a mistake to pay off terrorists," he said in a meditative tone. "It's a form of cooperation with the *fact* of terrorism, a reinforcement of the way of doing things. You pay ransom money, and you're saying, 'I recognize your right to lay claim to my money.' The minute I learned Theo had been taken, I called Raymond in Norway and tried to prepare him for the fact that most likely he'd never see Theo alive again."

"You tried to talk him out of paying the ransom."

Oscar ignored that. "Have you ever tried to raise twenty million dollars in eight hours, Gillian? That's how long the kidnappers gave Raymond. *Eight hours.* Don't you see? They *wanted* him to fail. That's all the excuse they needed to go ahead and do what they'd planned to do from the outset."

"Kill Theo."

He nodded. "Kill Theo. Those thugs got more money than they'd ever seen in their lives *and* the chance to maim and kill. A real red-letter day. They liked killing, Gillian, don't kid yourself about that. The killing was the main thing. The money was just a wonderful bonus. Well, now do you understand? Have I cleared things up for you?" In his paternalistic mode.

I was quiet for several moments and then asked, "Did you help Raymond at all? Did you contribute anything to the ransom?"

"Of course! What a question!"

"How much?"

A pause. "I don't recall the exact amount. Elinor would remember."

"You have three houses, Oscar. One in George-town, one in Dover, and one here. Only three million more."

He stared at me. "You haven't heard a word I've said."

The conversation was clearly at an end. In the un-comfortable silence I got up and left the kitchen with-out thanking Oscar for the omelet or even saying goodbye; such amenities seemed pointless.

I sat down at the bottom of the stairway leading to the second floor and tried to still the butterflies in my stomach. It had been an unpleasant scene; neither one of us had really reached the other. Oscar was un-doubtedly right about the futility of paying off kid-nappers and terrorists. But when it's a member of your own family whose life is at stake, how can you take the chance? I didn't know what the answer was.

Nor did I know what to do next. I stood up and glanced up at the top of the stairway, as if the answer would somehow appear there. Elinor was still ill; and as much as I thought I ought to talk to her, I couldn't bring myself to go badger a sick woman. It didn't re-ally matter anyway; she'd just tell me the same things Oscar had told me. Nor did it matter the exact amount the Fergusons had contributed to Theo's ransom. Whatever it was, it wasn't enough.

A door opened and Nancy Younger came out into the hall. "Hello, Gillian," she whispered. "You're up early."

"I wanted to see Oscar before I went sailing. Do you know how Elinor is?"

"I looked in on her before I came down. She's pretty miserable. All she wants to do is sleep."

"Has a doctor seen her?"

A flush appeared on her cheeks. "Tom. Yesterday afternoon. He prescribed some antibiotics. I suppose he'll be back today?"

Asking *me*. I told her I supposed so and started to leave... when an unbidden thought popped into my head that made me freeze. I'd been going on the assumption that the family was collaborating on a Big Lie—the Matthew Zeitz story, made up out of whole cloth, to accommodate Connie and to stop me from poking my nose into something they wanted to keep hidden. But I'd made that assumption on the basis of *one phone call*—to the Boston police, right after Rob had brought the "good news."

But Rob had said the arrest had been made only an hour earlier. What if the record of the arrest simply hadn't had time to make its way to the desk sergeant's blotter or whatever he called it? *What if I had called too soon*?

"Gillian? Is something the matter?"

"I need to make a private phone call. Immediately."

My tone startled her. "Uh... there's no one in the study right now." She pointed to the room she'd just come out of.

I went into the study and closed the door behind me. I couldn't remember the rigamarole you go through to get long-distance directory assistance, so I had to look it up in the book. My hands were shaking and I had trouble finding the right page. What if I was wrong? What if I'd been mentally accusing the family of all these dreadful things when in fact they were totally guiltless? And Joel... Joel! Joel was exactly the innocent kid he appeared to be. I'd been in too big a hurry, I'd jumped to the wrong conclusion. Finally I got through to the Boston police...

... who neatly deflated my newly born hopes before they had time to grow any larger. I got the same answers as before, absolutely the same ones. No arrest of Raymond Decker's murderer. No Matthew Zeitz. No investigating officer named McCarthy. No way, lady. Our records are up to date.

Nothing had changed. Nothing had goddamned fucking bloody well changed. I was right back where I was a few minutes ago, stuck in the middle of a family that would go to any extreme to protect its only chance for perpetuating the bloodline. Joel Kurland, the Deckers' grand and glorious hope for the future! Survivor! Psychopath! Killer!

Hurrah. Hurrah.

FIFTEEN

WE LOST the *Ghosts* sketch.

When I got back, Connie was taking a call from Leonard and handed the phone to me with relief; Leonard sometimes affected people that way. Yale had got the sketch, he told me, to no one's real surprise. Leonard had bid "vigorously" but "slyly"—his words—but I had, after all, put a ceiling on the amount he could bid and there was only so much he could do. That sounded rehearsed; he'd probably already used the speech once before, on the museum's board of trustees. I was the villain for not allowing him to bid all the museum's assets on this one item; he was the stalwart hero struggling against unreasonable odds to achieve the impossible. Leonard told me Mr. Atkins wanted me to call him.

Atkins was one of the trustees; I called him as soon as Leonard was off the line. Mr. Atkins courteously inquired whether I would like to apply for an extended leave of absence; my assistant was qualified to take over if necessary. I told him I didn't anticipate being away much longer; there'd been several deaths in my family and certain problems had arisen. He said he understood and wished me luck in resolving said problems before too much time had elapsed.

The message was clear. My job was in danger. I'd have to worry about that later; the museum seemed very far away just then. "Where's Tom?"

"At the hospital in Oak Bluffs," Connie said. "An East Chop man's heart attacked him, and they called Tom. Complications of some sort and they wanted a specialist. Call Michelle, will you, Gillian? I've got to run—Mrs. Vernon will be waiting." And she was off to her full-time antihamburger job.

Michelle wanted to take the sailboat out right then, so I went over to her house. It seemed that only the twins and I would be aboard. Joel was going to a birthday party a little later in the day (thank god) and Rob had to attend to some business in Boston; he'd be back by nightfall.

"*One* of you had to go to Boston," Annette laughed.

Michelle smiled. "It was a fair toss."

Annette was wearing red shorts and a red tank top; she even had on red deck shoes. Michelle was wearing approximately the same outfit, but in white. I wondered how Annette happened to pick red as *her* summer wardrobe color; I'd have thought that was a winter color. But I appreciated the color-coding; it wasn't always possible to tell the twins apart without a little external help. "Have you two ever swapped places? Stood in for each other?"

The twins exchanged a glance and laughed. "A few times," Annette admitted. "But only in emergencies. The last was—oh, two years ago. I had a meeting in Boston I couldn't miss on the same day I was sched-

uled to play in a tennis tournament here. So Michelle
played in my place.''

"How'd you do?" I asked her twin.

"I won," Michelle said with a rueful smile. "But
then I lost my own match later that same day because
I was exhausted from the first one."

"I still owe you one for that," Annette said.

We had to drive to Edgartown where the boat was
moored in a slip at the yacht club; it was too large for
the boathouse behind the Kurland's place. Still,
Michelle told me it was just as well there were only the
three of us, because with more than three or four on a
thirty-six-footer it tended to get a mite crowded.

The boat was a sleek-looking Swan 36 with a Volvo
engine. The twins put me to work finding a place to
stow the ice buckets of wine and fitting food into the
undersized refrigerator in the tiny galley; there wasn't
one inch of waste space. Michelle powered up and
steered us out of the harbor; only when we were several minutes out did she cut the motor and the business of unfurling the sails began. Mostly I stayed out
of the way.

I tried to put my customary initial uneasiness at being on a sailboat out of my mind because I needed to
concentrate. But Michelle was so busy showing her
sister all the features of the new boat that I couldn't
find a way to bring the subject up. The twins had already shared everything; they both probably considered the boat as much Annette's as Michelle's. At one
point Michelle had me take the wheel to show me what
a finger-light helm felt like. It was true; I could turn
the wheel with one finger—no friction, no play. The

queasiness in my stomach wasn't too bad, but I was glad we were staying in sight of the shore instead of heading out into open waters. We were sailing in the direction of Chappaquiddick.

Michelle had promised me a long talk during this sail, but by the time we passed the lighthouse on Cape Pogue it was clear *she* wasn't going to introduce the matter. I waited until they'd done what was necessary to get the boat to sail south instead of east and then said, "All right, let's talk."

They both looked at me brightly, waiting.

Bull by the horns. "Why didn't you give Raymond the rest of the money he needed to ransom Theo?"

"But Gillian, we did give Raymond what we had in our personal accounts," Michelle said with a show of patience. "Everything else was tied up in the business."

"All right, then, what about the business? Why didn't you just take the money from there?"

Annette undertook to explain. "It doesn't work that way, Gillian. Do you know anything about ventures at all? Well, every year we look at hundreds of business plans, searching for those with just the right mix of personnel and product and market need. When we find one, we supply seed money, the first-round financing necessary for hiring staff, leasing space, developing prototypes, all the things you need to do when you're just getting started. But rarely is the seed money enough to carry a business all the way to the point where it starts turning a profit."

"Make that 'never,'" Michelle sighed.

"Right, *never*. So the business has to go through additional rounds of finding financing—how many depends on the business. Sometimes we'll put in further cash ourselves, if we think we have a hot company. But the most crucial moment of a new company's life is the day of the initial public stock offering. That's the moment all the nickel shares and two-cent options we got for our investment suddenly take on real value."

Michelle said, "Even if our agreement forbids us to sell our shares right away, we do get a confirmation of the value of our investment. Or not, as sometimes happens. But that's the day we find out whether we picked a winner or a loser."

I was wishing the boat would stand still. "But why would you want to sell your shares?" I asked.

They both laughed, not unkindly. "Oh, Gillian, that's the whole point!" Annette said. "We don't want to remain owners forever. We cash out as soon as we meet the profit goal we fixed for ourselves at the outset—when our million or two investment has turned into anything from twenty million to a hundred. The whole idea is to get out after five or six years so we can start over again."

"Start over?"

"New startup investments. New companies needing seed money."

"New profits," Michelle added.

I thought about it for a minute. "Okay, I think I see how it works. But how did that keep you from coming up with Theo's ransom money?"

"Timing," Annette said with a shudder. "The most incredibly bad timing imaginable. Three-fourths of our investment money was then spread out among four new businesses, all four of which were going public within two weeks of one another. That was bad timing in itself. *And*—this is important, Gillian—our agreements with all four companies prohibited our selling any Decker and Kurland shares for a specified length of time after going public." She looked a question at her twin. "A year?"

"Eighteen months in one case," Michelle said.

"And that's where we stood when Raymond's call for help came. If we could have sold off our shares right then, there'd have been no problem. But any sale we made would have been illegal."

The motion of the boat was beginning to get to me. "Then why not make an illegal sale? By the time it came to light, you'd have already transferred the funds to Raymond in Norway."

"Gillian," Michelle said forcefully, "they put people in *jail* for that." She shook her head. "There was just nothing we could do."

You could have gone to jail.

"Oscar said from the beginning that they were going to kill Theo," Annette added almost absently. "He was right, unfortunately." She gave herself a little shake and said, "What a depressing subject. It's over and done with now—there's nothing to be gained from raking it all up again. Let's have some lunch, talk about something else."

"I'll get it," Michelle said. "You take the wheel. Gillian, I'll need your help."

The subject was evidently closed. I made my way awkwardly to the galley entrance so Michelle could hand things out to me. I heard a soft *Oh*! from inside and looked in to see her sucking a finger.

"Cut myself," she said. "Now where is that first-aid kit?" She found it and put a Band-Aid on her finger.

One bright red drop of blood had fallen on her white shorts. "Better get that before it stains," I said.

Michelle hadn't noticed. She wet a sponge and went to work. "They say blood is one of the easiest things to remove if you get it right away. I've never found that to be true." She scrubbed away.

Eventually lunch was ready. The boat's constant motion combined with the briny smell of the water didn't do much for my appetite; I tasted the white wine and picked at the crab salad. The twins talked of this and that; Annette was saying she wanted to sell the house in Brookline and move to Dover. The sun was hot on my skin, and rivulets of sweat ran down my back. I was feeling a little woozy.

Think. I interrupted Annette's talk of houses. "You said three-fourths of your funds were invested in four companies due to go public. What about the other fourth? Why couldn't you use that?"

They both looked at me in exasperation. "Seed money for other companies," Michelle said slowly, as if speaking to a child. "Operating expenses. Insurance."

"What you're telling me," I said miserably, "is that the money was there, but you were unwilling to jeopardize the business even to save Theo's life."

"You don't *know* it would have saved him!" Annette snapped.

"You don't know it wouldn't have!"

"Annette," Michelle said softly, "you're wasting your breath. She just doesn't understand our business."

"Your business!" I cried, furious with them. "I understand what your business is! And what I understand is that you've gotten fat off other people's ideas—*that's* your business!"

"Gillian," Michelle said in a tone of remonstrance.

"Well, haven't you?" I went on, wanting to hurt them. "Have you ever had one innovative idea in your lives? You look around for talented people with no money and then buy your way in. You're in the business of *leeching*. You've done nothing original of your own—nothing!"

"Original?" Annette inquired archly. "Like directing other people's plays, perhaps?"

"Theater is a communal effort," I replied hotly. "Everybody contributes. You ought to try it sometime."

"Oh, this is too much," Michelle said, provoked. "I don't know how much more of those holier-than-thou pronouncements of yours I can take. We buy our way in, you say? What do you call what you did with that museum of yours in Chicago? Gillian, you can't even get a *job* without buying it!"

A bucket of ice water in the face. I stared at them, unable to speak.

Annette was nodding. "We did a little checking up, once we knew where you'd been these past few years. You used Stuart's money to make a generous donation to the museum at the same time you were applying for the job of curator." She looked at me with contempt. "You have this glamorous picture of yourself as some independent, creative free spirit, when the truth is you'd have been waiting tables or on welfare if it hadn't been for Stuart's money. And you dare criticize *us*? What a hypocrite you are, Gillian."

My mouth was too dry to speak. I took a swallow of wine, now warm, and said, "Detectives. You hired detectives. To check on *me*."

Michelle lifted one graceful shoulder, let it fall. "Gillian, you were Stuart's wife, and that means there'll always be a place for you in the family. But you're hardly in a position to pass judgment, are you? So we'll have no more accusations or name-calling, is that understood?"

A charged silence descended. The twins were staring at me with something very like disgust... and suddenly I was afraid of them. I was out there alone on a boat with two women who'd let their brother's son die rather than do anything that might hurt their goddamned precious business. And they knew all about me. *All* about me. Shakily I moved away from the twins; I didn't even want to look at them. I curled up in the prow, seasick and wretched, and stayed there while they turned the boat around and headed back home.

I had never felt so desolate in my life. Michelle and Annette were right about me; I was a failure. All those years in the New York theater...it had taken me a long time to face up to the fact that whatever talent I had was minimal. Simply wanting a thing badly wasn't enough. The Deckers had never been cursed with the kind of uncertainty I was living with then; I felt totally lost. This was one show I wasn't directing; I didn't even know the script.

If it hadn't been for Stuart's legacy, I'm not sure what I would have done. Now I had a nice home and good work...but I hadn't *earned* any of it. At the time, it had seemed like a smart move to make a large donation to the Chicago museum, neatly cutting out the penniless Leonard in his bid for the curatorship. I'd even managed to soothe my conscience by telling myself I'd do a better job than that constipated little wimp, which was true. But it was still a shameful secret.

Only now it was no longer a secret. Did Tom know? Of course he knew; they all knew. Maybe they hadn't told Connie, but everybody else would know. I was ashamed. And the irony of it was that right now good old Leonard was in the process of stealing that very job I'd acquired by less-than-honorable methods.

It was late afternoon by the time we pulled into the yacht club slip. The twins did make some effort to talk to me; I answered in monosyllables. Michelle dropped Annette and me off at the compound and then drove away; she was picking Rob up at the airport.

Annette locked the gate behind us. "Gillian—"

I turned my back on her and walked away.

THE DAY HAD WORN me down, and I wanted nothing more than a cool shower and a soft bed. I found Connie in the kitchen making brownies with Joel, back from his birthday party and bored with sitting alone in an empty house. They had the radio tuned to the island's only broadcasting station, which was playing Beatles tunes as if they were brand new. It was a homey scene, but I was too depressed to join in; I told them I was going to my room. Joel followed me upstairs uninvited, demanding to know how I liked their new sailboat.

"The boat's a dandy, Joel," I told him. "The trouble is me. I'll never make a sailor."

"Sure you will," he said with conviction. "Everybody in the family sails."

"Your Uncle Raymond tried to teach me once," I said, remembering. "But even he was ready to give it up as a lost cause."

"Really? He's the one taught me. All us kids."

"A man of infinite patience."

He made a face. "Well, *almost* infinite."

"Almost?"

"Yeah, except when he blew his top, he *really* blew." He broke off sharply.

"When was that?" He didn't want to answer. "Joel?"

"Oh, that time, you know, when Theo got killed. He got mad at the family."

"At the family? About what?"

"The money," he mumbled.

It was like pulling teeth. "The ransom money?"

"Yeah. He was really steaming there for a while. So, when're you going sailing again?"

A real subtle change of subject, that. I looked at him, this boy, this probable cousin-and-uncle-killer, if I could only convince myself. "Do you miss Raymond?" Casually.

Joel shrugged. "Sure."

Did he? *Could* he? "Joel, I'm tired and I'm sweaty and I want a shower and a nap. I'll talk to you later, okay?"

"Okay," he said amiably and went back downstairs to Connie and the brownies.

I took something to settle my stomach and stood in the shower for a long, long time, relishing the feel of the cool water on my head and body. So Raymond hadn't been fooled by the family's excuse-making; seemed to me if anyone had a right to be furious, he did. While I was drying off I noticed my skin had that particular pinkish tinge that means a bad sunburn unless you do something fast, so I slathered myself with Noxema.

Once again, it took several minutes to understand the significance of something Joel Kurland had let slip; I was just lying down when it hit me. I jumped up and threw on some clothes and ran downstairs. A quick look around told me Joel was gone; a plate holding exactly two brownies sat on the kitchen counter. I found Connie out on the back deck, watering three plants I'd never seen before.

"Oh, Gillian...look at these! Aren't they pretty? They—"

"Connie, listen to me. I have to ask you a disturbing question. Put that down so you won't drop it." Wondering what I was taking about, she lowered the watering can to the deck railing. "I'm sorry as hell to have to bring this up, and I wouldn't if it weren't so important. Connie, I want you to tell me what Raymond did when he found out he couldn't raise all of Theo's ransom money."

In an instant her face crumpled and she started stuttering and mewing; just like *that* the new Connie had regressed to the distraught, incoherent woman who'd first met me at the door of the Beacon Hill house. How frail her defenses were! I swore at myself for being so blunt and grabbed her by the arms. "Connie, listen! Get hold of yourself! Don't do this! Take a deep breath, count to ten."

She did, and I kept talking to her—not the way we'd all talked to poor, fragile Connie but the way I'd talk to a go-getter out to rid the world of junk food. It did the trick, because after a few moments she regained her composure and was able to talk without stuttering. "That was a terrible thing to throw at me, Gillian."

"Yes, it was, I'm a stupid woman, I should have led up to it. But, Connie, I still need an answer. I'm really sorry, but I *have* to have an answer."

She didn't ask why. "All right, I'll tell you." She swallowed. "He went crazy, Gillian! He scared me to death—I'd never seen Raymond act like that before! Shouting and making threats, breaking things. He'd calm down for a minute or two, but then his face would turn this horrible purple color and then he'd be off again. He was making all sorts of dreadful accusations, calling the family murderers and all... I didn't know what to do!''

"Did the rest of the family see him like that?"

"Oh, yes! They all few to Norway as soon as they could, and...well, Annette said he was just taking his anger and grief out on them because he couldn't get at the men who'd taken Theo. But he was completely irrational there for a while, and then I...I was sick for a couple of weeks, but by the time I got out of the hospital he seemed to be over it."

"No more rages?"

"No, no more. Every once in a while he'd mutter, 'Five million,' but that was all."

"Five million...dollars?"

Connie lowered herself gently into one of the deck chairs. "That was the amount the rest of the family contributed to Theo's ransom. They had only eight hours, you know."

Oscar had told me seventeen million of the demanded twenty had been paid. If the others had provided only five, that meant Raymond had managed to raise twelve on his own. Twelve million dollars in eight hours, over the phone, from a foreign country. Jesus. "Relations must have been pretty strained after that."

"Yes, they were for a while. But you know how Raymond always insisted the family was the most important thing—after a while things got back to normal. The twins and Rob went over the company books with Raymond when we all came back from Norway...to show him how the money was tied up? Rob tried to explain it to me, but I couldn't follow. Anyway, we all made the effort to forget what had happened." She looked at me hopefully.

Connie wanted me to forget, too, to make everything nice again. I truly regretted forcing her to relive all that horror, but she was the only one I could count on to tell me the truth. I bent over and gave her a hug. "I'm sorry, Connie. I won't bring it up again. I promise."

That was what she wanted to hear. She laughed and said, "You smell like Noxema! Oh, Gillian, I'm so glad you've come back! You belong here, you know."

I turned away so she couldn't see how the thought of that shook me. It shook me, because she might be right. Maybe the way I went about things wasn't so different from the twins' way after all; the significant difference was that they were better at it. They'd knocked my morally superior perch right out from under me that afternoon, and the fact that I'd had it coming didn't make it any easier.

Mrs. Vernon had given Connie the evening off, so the two of us stayed in alone. Tom called to say it would be hours before he'd know whether his patient was out of danger or not, so he was going to stay at the hospital overnight. Connie was back to being the new Connie and chattered easily about this and that. I'm afraid I wasn't very good company.

Because now that I understood what had happened here, I was all but paralyzed by the knowledge. It was so obvious, and so painfully inevitable—the only thing that could have happened. For the first time I understood why the kids had been killed, and Raymond. And who had done the killing. It wasn't Joel at all; I'd actually been willing to label that kid a psychopath rather than acknowledge what had been staring me right in the face all the time. It was so nauseating I couldn't bear to think about it. But I couldn't *stop* thinking about it. After a while I told Connie I wasn't feeling well and went up to bed.

But not to sleep, not even with the help of pills. Willing myself to relax didn't work; it almost never did. I heard Connie come up and go into her room. The clock said midnight. Then one o'clock. Then two. This was no good; I was just getting tenser and more wrought-up by the minute. I got up and dressed.

Tom was still at the hospital. Connie didn't know anything. I didn't feel stalwart enough to take on two of them at the same time, so that ruled out the Kurlands and the Fergusons. But Annette was over there in her big house by herself. Annette, then.

Confrontation time.

I jogged along the eerily moonlit road past the cedar grove, past the Fergusons' place, and then around to the back of Annette's house. Everyone kept a spare set of keys hidden somewhere between the house and the beach; but try as I might, I couldn't remember where the Henrys had kept theirs. It didn't matter; I found a window with a screen I could remove and climbed in, like a thief in the night.

Up the stairs to the second floor. Frontal attack: I opened the first door I came to and turned on the lights. The bed was empty. So was the next one I tried. But in the third room I hit the jackpot; Annette was sleeping in that bed all right.

And so was Tom.

SIXTEEN

I STOOD LIKE A STATUE inside the bedroom door. Tom and Annette went through a one-two-three response to my headlong intrusion. One, they squinted against the sudden light; two, they focused on me; and three, they reacted. Annette was out of bed in a flash, pulling on a wrap of some sort. Tom tried to speak to me, but he couldn't seem to get the words out.

Annette could, though; I don't believe I'd ever heard her speak so rapidly before. She was telling me to stay calm and not get excited and we could all sit down and talk this over like civilized human beings and more garbage like that. I felt as if someone had just driven a fist into my stomach. But at the same time the situation was inherently ludicrous; the Wife trying to reassure the Husband's Lover that everything was going to be all right.

It was a setup. The whole damned thing had been a setup—Tom's pursuit of me, the seemingly natural banding together of two semi-outsiders against the clannish Deckers, the alternating subtle and not-so-subtle pressures to hold me here where they could keep an eye on me. And all with Annette's cooperation...hell, she'd probably thought it up in the first place, she and her twin. I should know by now they were capable of anything.

"Well, you did it," I told them. "You surprised me. I thought nothing you could do would surprise me anymore, but you managed it. *The Seduction of Gillian*—a farce in one act." I looked at Tom. "Make that two acts."

At least he had enough decency left to look ashamed. But not Annette. "Gillian, I know how you're feeling—"

"No, you don't. You don't have the foggiest notion how I feel. You never did. But that's never stopped you and Michelle from including me in your, your manipulating. You thought if you threw Tom at me I'd be more pliable, I'd stop asking questions and 'fit in'... as docile and unquestioning as Connie? Is that what you wanted? Too bad, Annette—it didn't work."

Tom spoke at last. "Gillian, don't judge—"

"I *will* judge," I said heatedly. "It's about time you people were held accountable for what you do. You really do think the rules of decent human conduct don't apply to you, don't you? You do *anything you want*—and you're affronted if you're ever expected to answer for it!"

"Gillian—"

"Don't 'Gillian' me. You disgust me. All of you. *All* of you." I turned and left.

I heard Annette murmur something to Tom and then she came after me. As I ran down the stairs she was right there behind me, calling my name. I tried the first door I came to but I couldn't get the damned thing unlocked.

"You *will* listen," Annette announced, placing the flat of her hand against the door.

I ducked under her arm and headed for the window I'd come in through. Annette climbed out after me. This absurd chase persisted until halfway down the beach stairs when Annette grabbed my arms from behind in a grip of iron and commanded me to stop.

I stopped. "This won't do you any good."

"Perhaps not. But at least you'll understand something of what we've been going through—I can make sure of that. Of course our throwing Tom at you was disgusting. Do you think we don't know that? Let's sit down, Gillian. Right here."

So we sat down on the beach steps, Annette still holding on to one of my arms. In the eerie moonlight she looked like a ghost sitting next to me. "Why Tom?" I asked her. "Why not Rob, or even Oscar? He's still a good-looking man."

She waved her free hand. "Tom was the obvious choice. You might be reluctant to carry on an affair with Rob or Oscar right under their wives' noses."

"*Might* be? Thank you very much. So if it had been Michelle who went off to Paris instead of you, Rob would have developed this sudden interest in me—not Tom? You and Tom never were planning a divorce, were you?"

"Oh, there were thoughts of a divorce at one time, but the problems have been resolved."

"I'm so happy for you."

She sighed. "You have a right to be sarcastic, I suppose. You first learned of the divorce from Connie, didn't you?"

"Yes."

"She still thinks the divorce is on. We were going to tell her things had been straightened out, probably on the day of Raymond's funeral—we thought a piece of good news might make her feel better. But then you showed up and started asking all these meddlesome questions. We thought a little romancing might divert your attention."

"And Tom the Stud obliged. Tom the tomcat."

"Don't be too harsh on him—it was a desperate measure on our part. The whole thing was a stopgap plan, conceived in haste . . . to buy some time until we could find out what you were going to do. What *are* you going to do, Gillian?"

"Go to the police.

"About *Tom*?"

How aggravating she could be. "Of course not."

Her hand tightened on my arm. "You mustn't go to the police, about anything. I mean, you *mustn't*."

"You're hurting my arm."

"I'm sorry." She withdrew her hand, a Band-Aid on her forefinger scraping lightly across my skin. "But you must forget about the police, Gillian."

A Band-Aid. On her finger. The same Band-Aid I'd watched her apply on the sailboat, when she'd cut her finger in the galley while preparing lunch. I thought of the one bead of bright red blood dropping down onto her shorts.

Onto her *white* shorts.

White. White shorts.

"You're Michelle," I said stupidly. "You're not Annette—you're Michelle!"

There was an intake of breath, and then a groan. "We can't keep anything from you. What gave me away?"

Good god in heaven, was there *nothing* she would stop at? "The bandage. It wasn't Annette who cut her finger. My God, Michelle—you don't recognize any limits at all, do you? Your twin sister's husband!"

Her face was a white blur in the moonlight. "Oh, Gillian—*think*. Annette's house. Annette's bedroom. Annette's husband." She put her hand back on my arm. "But no Annette. Where do you think Annette is right now?"

I stared at her.

"That's right," she nodded. "She's with Rob."

My head began to reel. Husband-swapping! That struck me as hilarious and I began to laugh. Husband-swapping—how *very* suburban! John Updike would have loved it. I laughed and laughed. Maybe Tom was Joel's father and Rob had sired Ike—no, that wasn't likely; the twins would have arranged even that to their liking. I couldn't stop laughing.

"Gillian! Stop it! *Stop it*!"

Gradually I let my laughter trail away, even though I still thought it was all so very funny. "I know you and Annette share everything, but it just hadn't occurred to me that 'everything' included husbands as well."

"We share families, not just husbands. Do you think either one of us would marry a man who was a stranger to the other?"

"What?"

Michelle made a sound of exasperation at having to explain something so obvious. "I married first, you know. But Rob and I didn't go ahead with it until Annette had substituted for me a few times in the, ah, premarital bed. We had to know whether she found Rob compatible or not."

"Compatible!"

"Yes, compatible. Then when Annette was thinking of marrying Tom, it was my turn to check *him* out. It was the only sensible thing to do, Gillian, since we knew we'd be sharing." She laughed easily. "The men didn't even know. They learned to tell us apart quickly enough, but at that time they couldn't."

I stood up and moved down a few steps; I didn't want to be near her. "Did they ever find out you'd *tested* them?"

"Oh, we told them. Later."

"And they didn't mind?"

"No, why should they? They both passed."

That did it. That's what really made my stomach heave. There was just no end to it. They had their rules and the rest of the world had different ones, and if you didn't like it—well, tough shit. Michelle was so *calm* telling me all this; she was enjoying it, really enjoying it—since I was so obviously anything but calm. Rubbing my nose in it, she was. Treacherous, amoral, *poisonous* people! I turned and ran down the steps to the beach.

I could hear Michelle calling Tom, and then another set of footsteps thundered down the stairway. He must have been on the rear deck listening, all this time. I ran and ran, digging my heels into the hard-packed sand; I had no destination, no plan. I just wanted to get away from *them*.

Tom finally caught me. He wrapped his arms around me from behind, making me stagger so that we both almost fell. They weren't the arms of a lover holding me now but those of a stranger; I didn't know this Tom, I didn't know him at all. "Don't struggle so, Gillian," he said, panting. "You'll hurt yourself."

"Oh, you're worried about my getting hurt?" I gasped. "Gee, that's real swell of you, Tom."

"Please, Gillian—don't."

Michelle came jogging up, breathing easily. She stopped and rested one hand on her hip, looking at me with an expression I couldn't read in the moonlight. "Gillian, Gillian. Whatever are we going to do with you?"

Was she asking for suggestions? "Drown me. Shoot me. That'll be easier than holding me prisoner the rest of my life."

"Now you're being melodramatic."

"Well, pardon me all to pieces. We can't have that, can we?" Responding like a child. Bitter? You bet I was.

Tom loosened his hold slightly. "You're not going to do anything rash, are you?"

I didn't think that worth answering. "*Are* you going to kill me?" I asked Michelle.

She acted shocked. "*Kill* you? Why would we do a thing like that?"

"That's the way you solve your problems, isn't it?"

"You don't know what you're talking about!"

"I know you killed Raymond," I hissed. Tom's hands tightened on my arms. "You two and Annette and Rob and Elinor and Oscar. All of you. You all ganged up on Raymond . . . and *you murdered him*."

For a long moment the only sounds were those of three people's harsh breathing and the slap of water against the shore. There—it was out in the open now. I'd made my accusation. The question was, what were they going to do about it?

After a while Michelle spoke one word: "Conference."

MICHELLE'S PLACE was the closest, so that's where they took me. I was tired, tired and depressed. Michelle went upstairs to wake her twin and her husband. Tom gave me a glass of brandy and laid a hand on my shoulder; I took the brandy but shrugged off his touch.

Annette was the first to come down, wearing a Chinese red silk robe with a red sash. She came over to where I was sitting and touched my face, gently. "Oh, Gillian. Why couldn't you leave well enough alone?"

Well enough? She called murdering her own brother *well enough*? I didn't answer.

"We can't let you leave now, you know." For the first time since I came back, Annette looked her age. "You do understand that, don't you?" I still wouldn't answer. She sighed and left me to drape herself decorously over the middle of a sofa.

Rob and Joel came down together, and I felt a whole new set of aches. I'd put all the blame on Joel, when in fact it was his...Joel! "What's Joel doing here?" I asked sharply.

"It's all right, Aunt Gillian," he answered sleepily. "I—"

"You didn't involve *him* in it, did you?"

"Don't be absurd!" Rob said angrily. "What do you take us for?"

"Then what's he doing here? Do you want him to find out—"

"He already knows. Joel has a right to know. It's part of his heritage, after all, grim as it is."

"You told him? You actually *told* him about it? He's only fifteen years old!"

He smiled tightly. "I know how old he is, Gillian."

I gave up on the father and turned to the son. "Joel? Do you understand what they did?"

He nodded. "Better than you do, I think. I understand they saved my life. They've risked everything they have to keep me alive. Yes, Aunt Gillian, I understand."

Michelle came in, announcing Elinor and Oscar were on their way. She was wearing the same robe she'd put on when she jumped out of bed in Annette's house—white. I'd been too stunned at the time to notice.

"What was she planning to do?" Rob asked his wife.

"Go to the police," Michelle told him.

"I'm right here," I said acidly. "Ask *me*."

"Sorry," Rob apologized.

Sorry. I fought down the urge to start laughing again. *Sorry.* Oh, by all means do let us keep our manners!

Tom spoke up. "Rob, I need to borrow a shirt." He was wearing only pajama bottoms.

Rob took him upstairs; I watched them go, wondering at the two men. They were partners in a conspiracy to commit murder, they shared wives as well as family life, they were thrown together in constant close cooperation not by their own choice but by that of Annette and Michelle. And now they would cooperate again, in deciding what was going to happen to me.

Elinor and Oscar came in, eyes puffy with sleep; Elinor carried a box of Kleenex. Oscar came over and planted himself in front of me. "So. You just couldn't keep your nose out of it, could you?"

"Oscar," Michelle said and shook her head.

He paid no attention. "This whole matter would have been over and done with if *she* hadn't come along."

Oh, *I* was the villain. "If you expect me to beg your pardon, think again," I snapped. "You're the ones who killed Raymond, not me."

Elinor interceded, her voice still hoarse from her cold. "It had to be done, Gillian. It was the only way to stop him."

"No, it *wasn't* the only way to stop him! You could have gone to the police!"

"With what?" Rob asked, coming back in. Tom followed, wearing not only one of Rob's shirts but a pair of his tennis shorts as well, which were too tight on him. "How could we go to the police?" Rob asked.

"We had no hard evidence. We knew Raymond had killed Bobby and Ike and Lynn, and he knew we knew. But we couldn't prove it. Doesn't it mean anything to you at all that he killed our kids?"

"Of course it does!" I cried. "How can you ask such a thing? But you don't murder people because they go crazy! Raymond was insane!"

Annette came up to stand by Oscar. "Raymond, I'm sorry to tell you, was in complete and constant control of his faculties. He was no more insane than you are. He knew exactly what he was doing. Raymond deliberately and coldbloodedly set out to murder all our children." Joel was listening to this tight-lipped and saucer-eyed. Elinor, who was nearest, placed a comforting arm around his shoulders.

And so finally the family's ugly secret was out in the open. Raymond never had forgiven the others for failing to come up with the money he'd thought would buy back Theo's life from the kidnappers. For a man whose whole existence was keyed to the solidity of a family base, the Kurlands' and the Henrys' and the Fergusons' failure to come through in time of crisis must have been unfathomable—as unexpected and inexplicable as the sun suddenly rising in the west or all the oceans of the world drying up overnight. He'd waited four years before finally figuring out what he was going to do about it; he had to have worked his way through many stages of his obsession before settling on his final, unmerciful plan. Raymond's whole idea of family must have gone through a full-blown reversal; nephews and nieces no longer meant anything to him other than a means of getting at their parents. Let *them* see what it was like to lose a child, and to lose one in such a grim and monstrous way.

I looked at Rob. "Back when you were feeding me all the various lies you'd thought up, you told me Raymond was the first to 'suspect' the kids' accidents weren't really accidents. Why did you tell me that?"

Rob snorted. "Because, believe it or not, it happened to be true. You see what Raymond's problem was? The killings had to be staged in such a way that the police would accept them as accidents, but *we* had to be made to understand that they were not. His revenge would be less sweet if we thought it was nothing more than random bad luck that had destroyed the kids."

So Raymond embarked on his scheme to teach the rest of the family a lesson. He'd waited in plain sight on the Vermont slope he knew Bobby Kurland would be skiing down. He'd bought a stolen car in Toronto to run down Ike Henry. And Lynn Ferguson had innocently opened the door of her hotel room, pleasantly surprised to see her Uncle Raymond in New York. What he'd had planned for Joel was not known. Then when he thought the timing was right, he'd planted the idea of murder and had the pleasure of watching them suffer.

But little by little, the various members of the family began to suspect the truth. They did some checking among themselves and found that Raymond's whereabouts could not be established for the times of any of the killings. The motive was painfully obvious to all of them. And Raymond had been ... different, ever since Theo died. More remote. Less giving. On the surface, all was well. But Raymond had changed.

After the third death, Lynn's, they were sure. Raymond had said he was going to Atlanta to look into a new investment possibility, but he hadn't checked into his usual hotel. They'd called every hotel in Atlanta; no Raymond Decker had registered in any of them. About that time Raymond had begun to suspect that they were on to him; he grew restless and apprehensive. When the tension got to be too much for him, he'd fled to Martha's Vineyard.

So they'd decided to confront him. Elinor invented some errands to keep Connie in Boston and Joel was still in school, but everyone else headed for the island. Raymond was close to the breaking point; killing his own kin had put a greater strain on him than he'd anticipated. When faced with six unrelenting, accusing relatives, he'd not denied what he'd done. In fact, he eventually reached the point of boasting about it.

"He knew he was going to die," Oscar growled. "Maybe he even wanted to die. He taunted us about what he'd done. He *taunted* us!"

I asked, "Didn't you consider going to the police at all?"

"Oh yes," Oscar said with distaste. "About a hundred times we considered it. But all we had was our conviction that Raymond was guilty—the police want more than that."

"There were other considerations as well, Gillian," Elinor said in her hoarse voice. "What would Joel's life at school be like if everyone knew his uncle had murdered his brother and two cousins? What would happen to the family business? And Oscar's career would be ended, that was certain.''

"So it wasn't *just* to protect Joel."

"Gillian, do make *some* effort to understand," Elinor rasped. "If we went to the police, about the only thing that *wouldn't* be hurt is our philanthropic foundation—nobody's going to turn down free money. But everything else would be gone—the lives we've built for ourselves, Joel's future . . . all because we were too gutless to take care of family problems ourselves?''

That was the real reason, I suspected. Everyone there must have been horrified at the thought of making this family disgrace public. Of course they'd want to take care of it themselves, so that's what they'd done. They'd talked it over and decided Martha's Vineyard was as good a place as any—better, in fact, than most. With the island's history of no homicides, the Vineyard police wouldn't be so quick to suspect foul play as, say, the Boston police would. So Tom had given Raymond an injection of something to knock him out, and then they'd set the fire.

I looked at Tom. "'First, do no harm,'" I quoted. He turned his head away.

"Unfair, Gillian," Annette said softly. "Tom was the one who resisted the longest, who looked the hardest for another solution. And he's suffered the most because of it. He was the one who wanted the divorce—not I." She sat on the arm of Tom's chair and rested a hand possessively on his shoulder. "It wasn't just me he was divorcing—it was the whole family. He even told Connie and Joel he was leaving. But then he started seeing things in a different light.''

I'll bet. "You talked him out of it.''

She raised one elegant eyebrow, a smile playing around her lips. "No.''

Tom turned his anguished face toward me. "I talked myself out of it. I'm every bit as responsible for Raymond's death as the others are. They have to stay together and live with it—why should I be the only one to escape?'' He pressed his lips together. "We had to stop Raymond, and we had to do it before he could get to Joel. If there were any other way, we'd have found it. This is my family, Gillian. I can't run out on them now.''

So when it came down to it, Tom couldn't break away from the Deckers after all. They had a lock on him. Forever. "Who set the fire?''

"*We* set the fire,'' Michelle said.

That was probably the only answer I'd ever get. It was enough; it didn't really matter who'd actually struck the match. It was a family killing, and the family that slays together stays together. I was tired, helplessly tired. "Why did you hire private investigators when you knew it was Raymond? Window dressing?''

"Pretty much,'' Michelle acknowledged. "Three deaths in a row—it would have looked odd if we *hadn't* hired detectives. We informed certain key people like Patrick Underwood, to help plant the idea that an outsider might be involved.''

"An outsider—someone like Matthew Zeitz?'' I asked. "Whose dumb idea was that?''

"Mine," Rob said, surprised. "You believed it, didn't you?"

"For about an hour. Then I called the Boston police and checked."

They all exchanged rueful looks. Tom asked, "Is that why you were throwing up in my bathroom?"

I didn't need to be reminded of that, so I asked him a question. "What was the gun for?"

"A prop. It's never even been loaded."

"Nor mine," Oscar said. The others all murmured agreement.

I was amazed. "You *all* have guns?"

"Of course," Annette said. "Empty ones. You were making noises about how we weren't taking adequate steps to protect ourselves. We knew sooner or later one of us would have a chance to show you a gun."

Was there anything they hadn't thought of? "You must be wrong about Raymond's sanity," I muttered. "A man has to be thoroughly sick to do what he did."

Elinor coughed a couple of times and said, "I'm growing a little tired of all this concern for *Raymond*. Since you couldn't be bothered having children yourself, Gillian, you have no idea what it's like to see your child struck down. Stop sentimentalizing Raymond. I won't stand for it."

"Yeah," Joel piped up unexpectedly. "Don't you like kids, Aunt Gillian?"

"I agree with Elinor," Rob said quietly. "You've done nothing but judge us since you came back."

"Well, somebody had better judge because all you're doing is making excuses for yourself. Look,

I'm not sentimentalizing Raymond—murdering those three kids was evil and inexcusable. I just can't accept that your solution was the only possible one . . . for crying out loud, you've turned yourselves into *killers* because of him!"

"There," Rob said. "That's judging."

Oscar pitched in. "Gillian, we had a horrendous problem dropped into our laps and we took care of it in the way that would hurt the fewest number of people. One—Raymond. It's easy to go all squeamish and dainty after the fact. You never had to face it."

"You're saying all the things you're supposed to," Annette remarked dryly. "'Oh, you terrible people, you actually killed Raymond!'" Her mimicry of my voice was unpleasantly accurate. "You're so conventional, Gillian. You're supposed to be shocked, therefore you are shocked."

"I have every right to be," I said shakily. "Of all the horrors committed in the name of family, this has to be the worst."

"Where did you get the right?" Michelle asked in a tone of honest curiosity. "You, the expert in running away from problems! You desert the family, you lie to yourself, you bribe an impoverished museum—"

"Whoa!" I stopped her. "You're not going to say my cheating to get a job is the same as *murder*, are you?"

"I'm saying you're hardly qualified to cast the first stone, are you, now—Gladys?"

Gladys. That stopped me cold; I hadn't known they knew. But they'd had me investigated. Probably even before Stuart and I...Jesus. Was there anything about me they *didn't* know?"

But Joel hadn't known. "Gladys? What's this Gladys stuff?"

The others made a point of leaving it to me to answer him. "It's common practice in theater," I said stiffly, "changing your name."

Joel looked amazed. "Honest? Your name is really *Gladys*?" He snickered. "Aunt Gladys."

"Enough of this," Elinor said in a tone of hoarse authority. "Gillian, you know you can't go to the police. You have no evidence. They'll treat you like one of those pathetic people who are always pestering the authorities with news of imaginary crimes. The worst you can do is embarrass the family. I think it's time you resigned yourself to staying here with us *where you belong*. It's time you started accepting the responsibilities of being a Decker."

"You want to make me an accessory after the fact," I said bitterly. My head sank forward to my chest. I was so tired.

The twins came over and crouched down beside me, one on each side of my chair. I felt their touch on my arm, my shoulder, my knee. "We want you to put all this behind you," one of them said; I didn't look to see which one. "We want you to stay with us always."

"Yeah, Aunt Gillian—stay." Oh, thank you, Joel.

I heard Oscar making some pronouncement about the museum's not being challenging enough work for me, and Elinor murmured something about the foundation's making a donation to compensate for my abrupt departure. The twins were trying to decide whether I'd be happier right in Boston or in one of the outlying towns. Rob said that could wait; I would take turns living with all of them for a while. They were planning my life for me.

I said I had to go to the bathroom; the twins helped me up as if I were an old lady. When I was finished, I stood outside the living room listening to the murmur of their low, cultivated voices; they were talking about investing some money in a play, or possibly even a new theater. They wanted me to be happy.

And suddenly I knew I couldn't go back into that room. I couldn't just give in to them; it would be like saying *Yeah, there are times when it's okay to kill*. I had to get away from them—now, right now. If I didn't go now, I'd never get away.

I slipped out a side door, trying to think what to do. Connie would be no help; she wouldn't believe a word of what I said. I didn't have a key to the compound gate, and there was no way I could get over that big wall. So the only way out of there was by water. I fumbled my way down to the beach.

The Kurland's boathouse was locked, as I'd expected; they wouldn't have left the keys in the ignition of the motorboat anyway. I left the pier and started along the beach toward Connie's house. So far as I knew, her boathouse hadn't been unlocked once in the time we'd been on the island; but I knew where she kept all her keys and there ought to be *something* in that boathouse I could use—a dinghy, a rubber raft. But finding the keys and getting back down to the beach was going to take time and I didn't know how much I—

Pain! I let out a yelp before I thought; I'd banged my shin against something on the beach. I rubbed my shin with one hand and felt around with the other. What I'd run into was a sailboard Joel had forgotten to put away.

A sailboard. Was that my way out? Just then I heard one of the twins calling to me from the house; they knew I was gone.

I kicked off my shoes and pushed the board into the water—*hurry, hurry!* The water was so cold a shock ran through my system; I ignored it the best I could and pushed farther out. While I was struggling to uphaul the rig I could make out figures moving down the steps to the beach. I finally got the sail in position and tried to think what to do; if I could just make it to Vineyard Haven, I'd be safe. But my mind was blank; everything Joel had taught me was gone.

They were at the waterline now, calling to me to come back. I fought with the sail, trying to force it to catch enough wind to give me some control. It bellied full for a moment, just long enough to carry me a little farther out; the figures on the shore were tiny, their voices no longer audible.

The black water was choppy and chill. Soon I was thoroughly drenched and numb with the cold. The sea pitched me back and forth, laughing at my efforts to find a trench between the waves. I began thinking that if I were spilled into the water this time, I might never come up. What the hell was I doing? Out on the Atlantic Ocean in the middle of the night, doing battle with an intractable sailboard in some harebrained, melodramatic attempt at flight? Insane, insane! A swell picked up the board and almost set it on end; I screamed as I felt my feet slipping out from under me. But the board righted itself just in time, and I narrowly escaped being dumped into the water. Thoroughly terrified, I let go the boom and squatted down, wrapping my arms around the mast and holding on for dear life.

By then I could no longer make out the figures on the shore. They could have come after me in the motorboat, I supposed, but maybe the water was too rough for even a powered craft. Or maybe they were hoping I would drown. That would solve their problem.

I was so afraid I would have screamed again if I'd had any voice, but it seemed to have deserted me. My legs and arms were cramping; the mast was slippery and I was having trouble holding on. I was so cold I lost my sense of touch. Every time I tried to breathe I got a mouthful of seawater. Eons passed.

Then, slowly, the wind and the water started pushing me back toward shore.

Forget about Vineyard Haven; I'd never have made it. There was no escape, and I should have known that. I was going back to the Deckers. The first voice I could make out was Joel's, yelling words of encouragement and something else about shifting my weight. The others were saying useless things like *Be careful* and *You can do it*. I did hear Tom calling *I knew you'd come back!*

I wanted to shout *I'm coming back because I'm afraid*, but my teeth were chattering so from the cold I couldn't get a word out. Then all of them except

Elinor were splashing out to grab the board and haul it—and me—ashore.

Elinor had her cardigan sweater off and wrapped around me before I even got off the board. I couldn't walk; someone was saying my feet were like ice and then someone else was rubbing them gently. They were all hugging me and patting me; I heard Oscar rumbling *Smart girl, smart girl* over and over again. I don't know whether they honestly thought I'd come back of my own free will or whether they were pretending not to know I'd had no choice. Not that it mattered anymore. I was so tired.

"I'm glad you came back," Rob told me with a big smile.

"And I'm glad you're safe," one of the twins said. "You scared us, you know—taking off like that."

"Whoo-*ee* Aunt Gillian! Even I wouldn't go out on water like that in the dark!"

What amazed me was the fact that *they were not acting*. They were genuinely happy that I was all right, and they were equally pleased that I was back with them again. For I was back, there was no longer any question of that. With all its ugly secrets and its ruthless rules, this was my family, and I'd made my last attempt at running away from them.

But after the trouble I'd caused them, I couldn't understand their willingness to forgive and forget. "W-why?" I managed to stutter at last. "Why?"

A twin—Michelle, I think—put both her arms around me and smiled warmly. "Because you're *family*," she said.

A Sheila Travis Mystery

MURDER

at Markham

PATRICIA HOUCK SPRINKLE

The body of beautiful bad girl Melanie Forbes is found wrapped in an Oriental rug in an unused basement storeroom of Chicago's elite school of diplomacy, the Markham Institute.

Sheila Travis, new administrative assistant to the president, has years of diplomatic experience behind her. Though unfamiliar with the protocol for dealing with a murder in one's new workplace, her nose for crime pulls Sheila—and her eccentric Aunt Mary—into the investigation.

"A delightful new sleuth makes her debut here."

—*Publishers Weekly*

OTHER PEOPLE'S HOUSES

SUSAN ROGERS COOPER

In Prophesy County, Oklahoma, the unlikely event of a homicide is coupled with the likely event that if one occurs, the victim is somebody everybody knows....

And everybody knows nice bank teller Lois Bell who, along with her husband and three kids, dies of accidental carbon monoxide poisoning. But things just aren't sitting right with chief deputy Milton Kovak. Why were the victims' backgrounds completely untraceable? And why was the federal government butting its nose in the case?

"Milt Kovak tells his story with a voice that's as comforting as a rocking chair and as salty as a fisherman."

—*Houston Chronicle*

D · A · T · E

WITH A DEAD

D O C T O R

TONI · BRILL

Midge Cohen's mother has fixed her up again. What would it hurt to meet this nice Jewish doctor, a urologist even, and give him a try, she insists.

But all Dr. Leon Skripnik wants from Midge, an erstwhile Russian scholar, is a translation of a letter he's received from the old country. To get rid of him she agrees to his request. The next morning, he's found dead.

"An engaging first novel. A warm, observant, breezy talent is evident here."

—*Kirkus Reviews*